GO TO SLEEP

A Novel

by

D. P. Sloan

Spinetinglers
PUBLISHING

Go to Sleep
By D. P. Sloan

ISBN - 978-1-906755-75-1

Spinetinglers Publishing
22 Vestry Road
Co. Down
BT23 6HJ
UK
www.spinetinglerspublishing.com

AUTHOR'S NOTE

First off I want to say thanks for buying my novel. This novel has taken sixteen years to make and I'm proud of what it has become.

I want to say thanks to my wife Rachael for coming up with the main names, and for supporting me through this. Thank you also to my young sister Kailey for designing the book's cover. Thanks to my parents David and Sheila for making me who I am today. Thanks to my other brothers and sisters: Scott, Edward, Samantha, Leigh-Ann, and to the rest of my extended family.

For my Grandparents, God rest their souls.

Lastly thanks to rap music & horror movies for their inspiration.

To you, the reader – thank you and enjoy.

PROLOGUE 1
One Killer's Future is Another Man's Pain.

Jacob Kane was a good guy, a friend to anyone, a family man. But that all changed as he stood perched on what he called Hell - a scary structure overlooking Paisley and West Dunbartonshire. He was about to jump. He felt as though he deserved it. Thoughts ran through his mind; he was like the monsters he read about: Charles Manson, Jeffrey Dahmer, Jack the Ripper. It was time for him to end his sorry excuse for a life.

He took a step forward, breathed and began to let go, when a voice stopped him. A voice that felt good, his saviour or his demon.

He breathed and shut his eyes. It was time to begin.

PROLOGUE 2
Just a Dream…So Far.

Two brothers abused. One dream of murder.

They all sat the round the table: his mum, his dad and his little brother. His little brother smiled, he smiled back.

The task had been done, the duty fulfilled. The Sunday roast lying in the middle of the table untouched, the steaming vegetables in the server bowl not empty.

His mum sat pale-faced, not talking.

His dad sat there with his head bowed.

He nodded to his younger brother, who handed him the knife back. The knife that had ended the abuse, the sadness and the pain. It dripped of blood. He held it up and watched as the blood slid down onto his hand. The hand that murdered his parents.

All was going to be fine, from here on.

He and his brother will lead a good life now. No more hiding, no pain and no sorrow.

He didn't show any remorse, he only smiled.

1
Zach Light
9th October 1992

He bounced down the stairs, big smile on his face; it was his birthday so time to celebrate. He was hoping he would get the new Nintendo game he was asking for and his birthday breakfast.

He bounced into the kitchen, still grinning from ear to ear, and then it all changed. There standing at the kitchen counter was his sorry excuse for a mother. A drunken alcoholic, a pill popper, a manic depressive and a sufferer from Munchausen's syndrome. The term Munchausen's syndrome is when a person intentionally fakes, simulates, worsens, or self-induces an injury or illness for the main purpose of being treated like a medical patient. Munchausen's syndrome is named after a German military man, Baron von Munchausen, who travelled around telling fantastic tales about his imaginary exploits. In 1951, Richard Asher applied the term to people travelling from hospital to hospital, fabricating various illnesses.

She stood there with her greasy hair and a bottle of vodka. At twelve years old, the boy knew his mother was twisted.

Go to Sleep

The boy sat down at the breakfast table. While his mum prepared his breakfast behind him he sat in silence, waiting, then he heard the cereal pouring into the bowl.

His mother poured the frosted flakes into the bowl and then picked up the sour milk (well and truly out of date). She poured it over the flakes, as it plopped into the bowl, she wasn't done yet.

Reaching for her valium, she crushed a few tablets with her glass of vodka and sprinkled them over the cereal while popping a few herself.

If she wanted to make him sick, she was going the right way. She slammed the bowl in front of her son and he just starred at it. Before lifting his spoon and taking a spoonful of it. This was just a ritual for his mother; this is how he became hooked on valium.

Valium was in everything: the food that he ate, the water that he drank, hell even the fucking peas on his plate. She sprinkled just enough of it to season his steak, so everyday he would have at least three stomach aches.

Now that's not normal right? What kind of mother would want to see her son grow up to be an underachiever? The teachers in the school also thought that he would amount to nothing. There was a time when his teacher shouted at him in class, "Zach Light stop sticking gum under the seat" The teacher called his mother up to the school one day and sat down with her. "Mrs Light, I believe your son is on drugs or something."

Obviously his sick and twisted mother wasn't going to explain to the teacher, that she was causing this. All she said that day was, "I'll take care of it."

The teacher arranged for the school nurse to do tests on him. "OK Zach if you just pee in this cup, all will be clear at the end."

The boy's response to this was rather abrupt. "No go fuck yourself!" Needless to say he was suspended from school; not once. not twice but literally every time. He was falling asleep in class. Mood swings would come out of nowhere. He would pick fights with anyone including teachers. The boy was turning into his mother!

The torture continued into his early teens. Same ritual: sitting at the dinner table waiting for his meal for the night. But when his mother placed the plate in front of him, he spoke back to her. "This is disgusting, I'm not eating that!"

His mother turned round and starred at him. "You ate it yesterday and I didn't hear no complaints did I? You are going to eat it and lick the plate clean! It's your fault I'm like this.

You and your fucking father's fault!"

He began eating it. His mum wasn't kidding, if he didn't eat it then it was more abuse.. Sheer torture, and to think she blamed him and his father. His dad got out fast when he and his little brother were kids. He had enough of the crazy bitch and just packed up and left.

There was a time he tried to get help outside by falling down and ripping his knee open, he was trying to get to hospital to get away from his mother – but it failed. Back home she hounded him for it shouting, screaming, "You've only got me you little brat, your dad doesn't want you, he doesn't send money to keep you!" His mum was simply a evil woman and his hatred grew bigger for her. She got him hooked on drugs and his life was changing dramatically. Nineteen years old and he was becoming a drug addict, he never thought he would become an addict. He kept saying, 'fuck-it, it'll never happen to me,' but that's actually what ended up happening. The past finally caught up with him. Any tablets became the way to go. He remembered one day he came home to find his dog dead. His mum sitting on the sofa, the dog in the kitchen: tongue hanging out, foam and blood at the mouth.

He stormed into the living room and stood in front of her. "What the fuck Mum! What happened to Freddy?"

She raised her drunken head and starred at him. "He had a headache so I gave him medicine!" She smiled at him. He grabbed hold of her bottle of vodka and threw it at the wall, smashing it into pieces. He slumped down in front of her only to see her standing up and head to the kitchen drawer shouting, "Here want a snack? You hungry you fucking brat? Look at that, it's a Xanax: take it and take a nap!" She walked back over to him and tried forcing it into his mouth. "Eat it!"

"But I don't need it!" he replied forcing her hand away.

"Well fuck it," she yelled. "Break it up, take a little piece and beat it before you wake Andrew up."

He grabbed it. "Alright Mum, you win. I don't feel like arguing!" He threw it into the back of his mouth, swallowed it and ran straight to his room.

2
Andrew Light
5th November 1999

Andrew sat upstairs in his room. Twelve years old, playing with his Teenage Mutant Ninja Turtles action figures. Once they were his older brother's but since he went off the rails, the toys became his.

He listened to the shouting, the arguing, the crashing, and the swearing. His older brother going at it hammer and tongs with the drug addicted, alcoholic thing he/they called Mother.

He had growing up not (really) knowing his father. Just waiting on the next argument between Zach and his mother. He knew what his mum was doing to Zach, as she tried to do it to him to.

Zach went off the rails due to the drugs his mum was putting into his food. Every time his mum tried to do it him Zach would take the plate of food or cereal from him and throw it in the bin while their mother wasn't looking.

Andrew played with his action figures, silently, listening to what was being said. He heard parts of the conversation, the bits where their dog was dead and where Zach finally gave in and took the tablets off his mum and swallowed them. Then he heard running up the stairs and Zach's bedroom door closing.

His mum plainly didn't want the boys. Andrew came home from school one day with a picture he drew of him, Zach, the dog and their mum. When his mum saw the picture, instead of smiling sweetly towards her son and pinning the picture up on the fridge, she tore it up right in front of the boy. Andrew started crying, and for crying he received a slap across the face. 'Go to your room you little bastard!' she had screamed at him. Not something a twelve year old boy wants to hear from his mother.

He ran straight to his room that day. But instead of sulking and hiding under his covers, he sat at his desk and grabbing a pencil and piece of paper. He began writing, I HATE YOU MUM, I HATE YOU MUM, I HATE YOU MUM over and over again. He filled the full A4 piece of paper and then grabbed another piece and began writing again. I WISH YOU WERE DEAD, GO TO SLEEP BITCH, DIE, DIE, HOW MANY TIMES CAN YOU RUIN OUR LIFE! The same thing over and over again. After finishing six pages he put them all together, and before he could put it away, he heard hard footsteps coming up the stairs. He raced to his hiding hole – the wardrobe, went inside and shut the door. He watched through the small crack between the doors as his mother barged in, holding her bottle of vodka in one hand. He watched her move across the room in one fast pace, and watched her pick up the written word he left there. She began reading it to herself and turning over the pages furiously. After disposing of it in the waste paper bin she flew to the wardrobe and yanked the doors open, to find her youngest son cowling in horror at the bottom of the wardrobe. She reached forward and pulled him up and forced him back into the bedroom.

She threw him against the desk and yelled, "You fucking wee brat! You think you can write that shit about me and get away with it?"

He began crying.

She starred through him with rage. "You little Jessie, you wee fucking girl. Maybe I should dress you up in dress and send you to school dressed like the little girl you are!" She slapped him across the face.

He threw his hands up to his face. "Please Mum no more. I'm sorry, I'm sorry, I'm sorry."

His mum kept slapping him not stopping until she drew blood.

The blood began to trickle down the right side of his face. "Zach!" he yelled. "Zach please help me!"

"Zach is comatose." His mother shouted at her young son. "He took enough of the tablets to sleep for a week!" She laughed. "You and him are fuck-ups just like your father. That prick left me with you two. So you deserve this!" She tightened her fist and punched him in the stomach. He bent over with the pain. "Now you can cry you little shit." She picked up the bottle of vodka and left his bedroom.

Andrew moved towards his bed but before reaching it, he collapsed in a heap.

3
William Light
15th January 1990

William Light, a well respected individual, a pillar of the community. At thirty years of age, he had it all: a wife and two young sons, one at ten years old and the other at three years old, and a recently built house, on two floors. William and his wife Sarah had their bedroom downstairs. The two boys' rooms were upstairs.

It all seemed like a perfect family, except for one thing – it wasn't. While William worked over forty hours a week, morning, noon and night, Sarah sat at home nursing either a sore back, sore legs or sore head. Pretty much anything was sore, day in day out. Anything and everything was wrong with her, so she had to either go to the doctors or to the chemist, or if it was major then the hospital.

William later discovered there was a name for what she had, after he was called by her doctor to go in and see him.

"Mr Light, your wife Sarah has what the medics call Munchausen's syndrome. It's where the patient imitates something they have seen either on TV or in a magazine.

18

Something they have heard from another person, maybe a friend or family member," the doctor explained.

William sat across from the doctor in a comfy chair. He leaned forward – puzzled. "Munchausen's syndrome?" He placed both his elbows on the desk in front of him and balanced his head on his hands. "You're telling me my wife is sick mentally?"

The doctor leaned back in his chair, arms folded he nodded his head. "Yes Mr Light, and if we don't treat her now, then through time she may try and do what she is doing to herself, to you and the boys."

William leaned back also folding his arms. "My wife wouldn't do that, she loves us all. For Christ's sake, she's only twenty-eight years old!"

"Age doesn't matter Mr Light," the doctor sadly said. "This could happen to anyone at any age. I do strongly will you to honour my wishes and get her help. She will be put through various tests. It'll be like a detox program."

"Doc – sorry," William began, "I can't do that to my wife, I love her. We will get through this." He stood up and began to leave.

"Your oldest son Zach – she's started to do it to him!"

William spun round, "What?"

The Doctor stood up, "Last week she brought him here saying he was going to sleep, then wakening up and jumping about as if he was hyper. He was also vomiting a lot apparently."

William shook his head, "You're being serious aren't you?"

The Doctor nodded.

William then turned, opened the door and walked out rather fast. He heard the doctor shout his name a few times but he didn't respond.

He arrived home and ran into the house. He found his young wife in the kitchen with a glass of water and what looked like small white tablets on the counter.

"What the fuck have you been doing to Zach?" he screamed, spinning her round and holding her forcely with both hands on her shoulders.

She looked gob smacked. "What are you talking about honey?"

His anger boiled up like a volcano ready to explode. He picked up the small white tablets. "These!" Reaching behind her, he opened up the kitchen cupboard and pointed to the vast volume of pain killers of all sorts piled high inside it. "And these!"

She looked him dead in the eye, "I have pain all the time and so does Zach. He needs his medicine just like I do!"

His anger erupted and for the first time ever, he struck her across her face, leaving an imprint of his hand in red down her right hand side of her face. "You stupid, stupid woman. You are going to kill our son and yourself if you carry on like this. I'm taking our sons away from you; you do whatever the fuck you want to do to yourself but not to our sons!" He walked passed her and into their bedroom. He grabbed hold of a suitcase from their wardrobe. He started packing his belongings. Fifteen minutes passed by and he had his belongings packed.

He left the bedroom and went down the hallway. "Zach, Andrew, come on boys."

He was met in the hall by his wife. "Where are you going?" she sneered.

"I'm leaving you!" he shot back.

She shook her head. "You'll come back."

He dropped his bags. "No, no I won't Sarah – it's over. Look, I feel so ashamed, I snapped. I shouldn't have hit you. I laid hands on you, I'll never stoop so low again, but this, us, it can't go on while you do this."

On that note William Light left the house, not even saying goodbye to his sons. It wouldn't be for a further ten years before he was to 'bump' into one of them again.

4
And Life Goes On
1st January 2000

This was just the beginning.

He lay awake in his bed, reminiscing about what has happened to him through his childhood and teen years. The physical, mental and drug abuse caused by only one person – his mother.

He moved out of his mum's house not long after finding out what she done to his younger brother. He tried his hardest to take his brother away from the house, but apart from the young one not wanting to go with him, he knew he was onto a losing battle.

Now he resided in a cheap bed-sit. A dirty stinking bed-sit he couldn't give a toss about. As long as he was away from her, that was the main thing.

One day when his dear old mother was knocked out via drugs and alcohol, he got out of his bed went into see his wee brother, who was just sitting in his bedroom looking out the window.

"Andrew – bro," he whispered. "I'm leaving, you want to

come with me?" Andrew just sat there silent. "Bro talk to me please," he asked again just a bit higher than a whisper. Yet again Andrew just sat there starring into space. A blank look on his face. "For fuck's sake man, talk to me!" he yelled. He knew there was no need to worry as his idiot of a mother wouldn't wake up even if the house was on fire!

Andrew turned towards his brother. "You said something?"

He sat down on the edge of the bed and placed his elbows on his knees. "Bro, it's time we left this god forsaken house!"

Andrew just shook his head, "Why?"

Zach just starred at his younger brother as if puzzled. "Why?" He was stunned by such a stupid question. "Andrew, our dear old mother is comatose! This will be the only time we get to get away from her!"

Andrew stood up taking one last glance out of the window. "No I'm staying. Mum is all we have now. Dad left what ten years ago! She may be is a drug addict and an alcoholic, but she's still our mum no matter what!"

He looked at Andrew, gob smacked. "You have me bro!" he exclaimed. "I'll look after you."

Andrew shook his head again, "No – Zach, you can't even look after yourself! No matter what mum does to herself and us. She'll always be our mum, if you want to leave then just leave, do what Dad done. Just go and don't come back!"

Zach's eyes went wide with shock, he couldn't believe his own brother, his only brother was saying this. Did he like the abuse that was handed to him? Did he enjoy it? Only Andrew knew. "Last chance wee man, you coming or not?"

Andrew turned towards the window again. "No!"

Zach stood up, shocked more than anything, and left the room. He didn't bother taking any belongings; he raced down the stairs and out the front door.

His first stop was to go to the council. He headed to another town just outside Glasgow, a town called Clydebank. As he entered the reception area late in the afternoon of December 21st 1999 he was met by a young woman at the counter. "Can I help you?" the young brunette with a cheeky smile said to him.

"I've been kicked out of my mum's house; I've not got a place to go. Can you help me please?"

The sexy receptionist nodded. "No problem, what's your name?"

He placed both hands on the counter. "Zach, Zach Light."

The young woman wrote down his name onto a piece of paper. "OK Mr Light, if you take a seat over there," she pointed to her left, "someone will be right with you from the homeless section."

He followed instructions clearly, and it wasn't long before he was taken into a small, office consisting of a desk and two chairs. He sat down and told his story, filled out forms galore and then waited. He explained that he had no clothes, no food, no furniture, no nothing and then he broke down. He didn't say that his mum was drug addict, an alcoholic and didn't say that he had a brother and that he was still staying there. All he said was simple and straight to the point. "Me and my mum don't see eye to eye and because it's her house, she threw me out, end of story."

The council officer understood, and as he sat out in the reception again, he waited patiently for what the council had to say. It took near enough thirty minutes before he was called back in. As he sat across from the officer again, she smiled at him.

"Good news Mr Light, the council are willing to house you, but only in a homeless unit. It's the blue triangle, are you aware of where that is?"

He nodded. "Yeah, it's here in Clydebank isn't it?"

The officer nodded. "That's right, just next to the train station. It's a bed-sit and has the basic amenities in the flat. We will put you on the waiting list for an actual house but that'll take a long while. Are you OK to go to the homeless unit?"

He nodded. "Anything to get off the streets, I couldn't face living on the streets."

The officer smiled a happy to help smile. "Well we will contact the social services for you and get you on council tax and rent benefits. All you need to do is go to jobcentre and apply for Jobseeker's Allowance, that'll keep you going for essentials OK?"

He nodded and then stood up. "Thank you again Maureen." He shook her hand and then left.

And now he sat starring up at his ceiling in his dirty stinking bed-sit, January the 1st in the year 2000, over the past week he had been having very vivid nightmares, wakening up in a cold sweat at 3 a.m. every morning. His dreams consisted of him standing over dead bodies, blood everywhere. Blood dripping from the knife clasped in his hands.

The nightmares leaked into his reality, maybe it had something to do with his upbringing, but he knew the only reason was the fact his mum abused him.

Was this was his way of coping with his abuse?

Was this his mind telling him to kill in order to stop this abuse?

He swung his legs over the side of the bed and just sat there, and then the tears came. "Mum you motherfucker, you fucked my life up, you fucking stupid bitch, I wish you would die!" Tears dropped onto his lap and he wiped them away.

He stood up and walked into the bathroom. He ran the bath and then stared long and hard into the mirror as it began to fog up with the steam from the hot water.

He went back into the sleeping area-come-living area and grabbed a towel and clean boxers. (The social managed to give him a loan to buy clothes and essentials. And his jobseeker's money topped up his food fortnightly as well.)

He went back into the bathroom and as he placed the towel and boxers down on a stand containing shampoo and deodorant. He turned towards the sink and mirror to grab his razor. And that's when he saw the words written on the mirror:

KILL YOUR PARENTS ZACH!

He mouthed the words, "What the fuck!?!" and then wiped the mirror clean. Shocked more than anything: gob smacked and puzzled.

He climbed in the bath (as it was still running) and then lay down, just after he turned the taps off. He shut his eyes and just lay there in total silence, listening to the drip, drip, drip of water from the tap.

He must have drifted off to sleep again and then dreamed

once more.

He opened up the front door of a house and heard screaming, he raced inside looking for where the screaming was coming from. He looked into the living room – nothing happening there. He raced passed the downstairs bathroom – nothing there either. Last stop on the ground floor - the kitchen. He stopped short of falling over as on entering he was met with, what looked like him standing over a woman's body. The woman was screaming, she was covered in blood. She was wearing only a white nightdress that stopped just above her knees. Her hair was matted to her skin, soaked in blood. He stood there watching 'himself' brandishing a black handled kitchen serrated knife. 'Himself,' turned to him and glared, "you know what to do!" He just stood there. "You're not real, this is a dream, it's just a dream!"

'Himself' just stood there. "This cunt fucked you up. You need to kill her and then your daddy!"

He shook his head. "Not real – not real, NOT REAL!!!"

'Himself' just smiled, a evil smile. He raised the knife and plunged it into the woman on the floor: once, twice and then the third time the knife went deep into her stomach and he pulled it up towards her breasts. 'Himself' turned to him again. "If you don't want to do it for yourself, do it for

Andrew. That little bastard is suffering more since you left him behind! Your dear mummy is fucking him – her own personal sex toy - and guess what? Your dear wee brother loves it!"

He shook his head, tears forming again at the side of his eyes. "You lie, you're a liar!" He lunged at 'himself, but 'himself' just disappeared along with the woman. He stood there, gob smacked. "What the fuck?" he whispered, before turning round and meeting 'himself' face to face. 'Himself' raised the knife, and as he cowered and protected his face with his arms, the knife came down and ripped through his flesh.

He jumped up out of his bath. Sweat pouring down him. Breathing fast, heart racing. He looked down at his arms and noticed the cuts all over them; blood seeped out of tiny cuts along his bare arms. He looked down into his bath water, which was now a nice shade of red.

He jumped out, grabbed the towel and tried to stem the bleeding, and that's when he noticed the mirror. More words were etched onto the mirror through the condensation.

CATCH THEM AND KILL THEM ZACH!

He grabbed toilet roll and dabbed at the cuts, it wasn't until the blood was cleared away that he noticed there was actual words etched into his skin as well. He bent his arm so he could read it. His eyes went wide with fright. His right arm bore the words;

EVIL SOUL

He grabbed his boxers, a few bandages from the cabinet and went into the other room. He dressed the wounds and contemplated what the hell just happened.

Why the dreams?

Why now?

He decided that he would tough it out, maybe it was due to the trauma that he was accustomed to earlier in his life. He decided to see what happens. But just put it down to vivid nightmares, surreal nightmares.

But nightmares can't harm you – can they?

Nightmares can't tell you what to do – can they?

Two questions that would haunt him, and this city, for a long time coming.

5
Sandra Light Loves You, Son
25th December 1999

Andrew, at such a young age, was being abused.

Christmas day in the Light house wasn't as special as other families' Christmases. There were no presents, no stockings, no turkey or Christmas pudding. Zach was now gone from the hell house, so it was just him and his dear old mother.

Andrew saw enough of his mother in him (figuratively speaking). He always thought, *what if I grew up to be like her?* What would his life end up being like? In usual cases, looking up to your parents was to inspire to be like them. But in Andrew's case that would be wrong on so many levels. Despite all the shit she put him through, for some reason, he still admired her. He was a depressed young boy and every time he felt this way the whole world was grey to him.

He just couldn't care less anymore.

Andrew sat up in his bed and waited; waited for his mum to shout on him, and on queue she did just that. "Andrew," she howled. "Andrew come in and see your mum. I need some help please!"

Andrew sighed and got up onto his feet. "There's a surprise!" he sighed. He walked out of his room and along the hallway and down the stairs towards his mother's room. He didn't bother knocking on the door, he just went straight in. There, lying on the bed completely nude was his loving mother.

"Come over here son," she asked nicely for some reason.

He made his way over and as he stood in-front of her. She swung her legs over the side of the bed making him stand in between them. "You know what Mummy wants don't you?"

He nodded.

"You know that you have to do this as a sign of your love for Mummy, don't you?"

He nodded.

"Lie next to me Andrew," she said.

He climbed up and over his mummy and lay next to her. His mum abused him and it wasn't the first time. He knew it was wrong, but it was either do it or be tortured. He had no one to turn too: Daddy was gone, and Zach was gone. He didn't want to take tablets or be punched again, so it was do this or get punched. He hated being hit – not that anyone was going to see him anyway! His mummy pulled him out of school and said she would home school him. The school board allowed that, and didn't see anything wrong with it.

Go to Sleep

Since Zach left Andrew was now her victim, her plaything. She abused him – physically, mentally and sexually, and found nothing wrong with it. In her eyes it was all good: she blamed her ex-husband, she blamed her eldest son. So now Andrew got what she said he 'deserved'.

Andrew knew it was wrong; he wanted to tell people what his mummy made him do. What his mummy did to him. The cigarette burns in his flesh, his food being spiked by all sorts of drugs. The exact same as she done to Zach.

Maybe one day, Andrew would be able to leave this God forsaken house, go and live with Zach and all will be better.

Maybe...just maybe.

6
Drugs Don't Work
19th January 2000

The sweating came on him extremely badly; he wanted his next fix as soon as possible. He had become addicted to all sorts of drugs; he tried going cold turkey, but only lasted two hours. More hatred for his mother and father poured from every hole in his body. His dear old daddy left him and Andrew with this thing that they called a mother. Now he was away from the hell house, but the craving for drugs just got more and more intense. He already got his jobseeker's money but that all went on electricity and food - all of twenty pounds worth, mostly made up of microwave meals, ten pence crisps and Irn Bru. The rest of his money went on drugs: cocaine, hash, blues you name it – anything he could get. He had spent all his money by 11 a.m. Now he was feeling the effects, he needed something almost for the pain as such. But with no money the next best thing was...to steal.

He walked down the pavement on his way to the local shopping centre, an old woman pulling her shopping trolley passed by him and looked at him with disgust. He snarled at her. "What you looking at you old bitch?" With shock and awe she tsk-tsk him and carried on walking. Or, as he thought, waddled down passed him. He was angrier now, how dare she stare at him as though he was a piece of shit? He turned on his heals and started following her; slowly behind her so she wouldn't suspect a thing. She was totally oblivious to him following her. She continued on her journey home (he gathered) - she turned left and walked down a lane, which was littered with garbage. (Hell what do you expect – you are in Clydebank after all!) He picked up his pace and on closing in on the old bitch, he pulled a small stainless steel serrated knife out of his pocket. (It was to threaten staff at the shops for when he was going to steal from them.) He got closer and closer and just as he neared her, she turned to face him – eyes wide with fright.

"Remember me!" he growled at her.

The old woman didn't say a word just stood there, shaking.

"You fucking old cunt you stared at me – you got a problem with me? The way I look? Fucking talk to me bitch!" he yelled at her, not too loud for people to hear.

"I'm...I'm sorry," the old woman stammered.

He just smiled at her. "Well I'm not!" He showed her the knife, and with such force he plunged it deep into her stomach two, maybe three times. When he pulled the blade out, the old woman tried to cower and cover her wounds but that didn't help her, and with rage in his eyes, he forced the knife again, but this time in to her sides and then started swiping the blade in slashing motion all over her arms. Then as she fell to the ground, surrounded by garbage, he raised the knife and plunged it deep into her left eye, but not too deep as that would have pierced her brain. He heard a *pop* noise as her eye juices flowed from her socket, and as he pulled the knife out he heard a voice saying, 'finish her!' - and he did just that. He raised the knife one last time and aimed it directly between her sagging breasts and forced it through her chest cavity directly into her heart.

He stood up and glanced down, but with no remorse he bent down grabbed the now blood covered dead woman's purse from her jacket pocket and then walked away, while checking the purse. "Jackpot!" he said to himself. "She must have just cashed out her pension." In the purse was four hundred pounds - he walked away a happy man.

First murder – drug dependency.

7
Police Officer William Light
21st January 2000

A pillar of the community, a police officer, and now standing alongside the chief of police at a crime scene so vile, so disgusting that even the pathologist puked up on inspecting the body. William Light stood next Chief Inspector Alex Grimm – a chubby man, in his mid fifties wearing a plain black suit with a black overcoat to keep the chilly January winter weather out of him. "This is just nasty!" Alex exclaimed.

William nodded. "Yeah sir, you can say that again," he began. "I mean yeah we have seen murders by the dozen here in these parts, but this is brutal!"

Alex bent down over the body and shook his head. "This is mental! To fucking do this to her, the slash marks, the eye gouging - that's taking it too far!"

William agreed and went and got the pathologist from the corner of the alley. There, kneeling down, wiping vomit from his mouth, was the pathologist, Doctor Curtis Knox. A small man in his mid sixties, wearing the infamous white polyester uniform.

"You alright Doc?" William asked.

The doctor nodded. "Yeah son – just not seen anything like that before. That was a brutal attack. There was no need to gouge out her eye!"

William agreed. "Listen Doc we need to get the body back to the morgue. The boss wants to know the cause of death."

The doctor nodded, dry heaved and then stood straight up, looking at the officer. "That's easy William, stabbed to death!"

William smiled. "Yeah I know that and you know that Doc, but you think he's going to just write down in a report, victim – stabbed to death!"

The doctor laughed. "You got a point, OK give me five minutes and I'll be over and we will get the victim moved.

William nodded and retreated back to his officer in charge.

Alex was just getting back into his car when William approached. "Sir, Curtis will be over in five minutes he's just getting himself together and then we will get the body back to the morgue for analysis."

Alex nodded. "Thanks William, listen I'm going to head home the now. Phone me once the analysis has been done okay?"

William nodded and then Alex was speeding away in his black BMW.

William returned to the pathologist who was back at the body, along with his assistant. After taking various photos of the surrounding area, both pathologists bagged the body and put it on a stretcher and into the back of their private ambulance. "William I'll call you with the results, or you can come down later?"

William cleared his throat. "I'll pop back to the station and start the report, let's say in about an hour I'll come down?"

The doctor nodded and both him and his assistant got in the private ambulance and drove away.

William stood there still, wondering who on earth could have done such a thing. Who could butcher an old lady and not give a damn about it?

His questions will be answered - ten years after he walked out on his sons.

His questions will be answered - after another few victims fall before him and the city.

8
What Have I Done?
25th January 2000

Lately he really felt like he was walking through Hell, he felt like he was losing control of himself. But life kept on being complicated, and he was debating on leaving this world. He was grieving, not because of what he had done, because of the pain he had been put through. He tried to hide it, but he just couldn't. He tried to act like he was all high and mighty, when really, inside he was dying.

He needed help, but knew he couldn't do it by himself, he was too weak. For months he had been having ups and downs, going through with the idea of ending the shit right here.

He hated his reflection; he walked around the house trying to fight mirrors, he couldn't stand what he looked like, he looked ugly, but so what, did he care? He didn't give a fuck, the only thing he feared was being caught, he was afraid of the consequences.

He locked himself in the bedroom, and sometimes the bathroom, he even napped at noon, and yes he was in a bad mood. He always spoke to himself, or the voices inside his head, saying, "Zach what happened with you? You can't stop with these pills. It's become a problem that you're too pussy to tackle, so get up, be a man, stand, a real man would have had this shit handled."

Now he was popping uppers and downers and methadone pills. And the fucking drug dealers hung around him like 'yes man'.

He had no friends who could understand him; he was starting to live like a recluse. The truth was sleeping pills would make him feel alright. And if he was still awake in the middle of the night, he just took a couple more, he wasn't slowing down for no one, sometimes he felt he would almost slip into a coma, all he kept hearing was the voices saying, 'Zach, don't you die on me. Zach, better hold your ground'.

He dreamt one night that he woke up in the hospital, full of tubes, but somehow he was pulling through. He swore when he came back he would be bullet-proof.

He still loved his mother and father, that would never change; but what they did to him is why he was on such a path of destruction. He thought about it every day, and he wished that they all could put it aside and move on but it was never going to happen that way now, he was in too deep.

He wished there was a better way for him to say it, but he

swore he would get revenge on everything that they had done to him. There were just too many things to explain, that being the reason he was doing this and why he was doing this.

He couldn't pretend there wasn't any blame to place on his parents, there was simply a lot to place on them, he was pointing fingers at them, and he knew he wasn't a saint growing up but his whole history just felt like it was pissed away. He missed the old times, the younger years and just didn't have anything else to say.

He was going through changes, and knew he was becoming a psychopath, a serial killer, and the game had begun once he killed the old woman.

He rocked back and forward on his filthy bed; thoughts going through his now disturbed mind. He had just murdered an old lady. Not just murdered her, but mutilated her, gouging out her eyeball and then stole her purse. OK, it's OK to kill somebody (well not really) but to mutilate them! To rip them apart! To make them suffer! No it wasn't OK! But he had to do it, he had to do something. Maybe murder wasn't the best option, but doing something was. He had become a monster, a monster addicted to drugs – a junkie none-the-less!

He rocked back and forth, wondering if the cops would know it was him, wondering if he would receive a chap at the door - 'Hello Mr Light, we would like a word with you regarding the murder of an old aged pensioner the other day.'

'I don't know what you are talking about,' would be his answer.

It had been seven days now since he committed the ugly and brutal attack on the poor defenceless woman, but only the tacky local newspaper picked up the story. It wasn't major news, after all it was only in Clydebank, the most famous part of Glasgow around: home of the John Brown's Shipyard and the Titan Crane. Clydebank suffered during the Second World War in 1941. Glasgow suffered during the 1960s when a killer struck the city centre, a killer nicknamed 'Bible John'.

But that was then, and this was now. He thought deep about what he had done and wondered was it really that bad? Was it on par with the war raids? On par with the 'Bible John' killings? No one had seen him. No one had come to his door, and above all else, he didn't leave any evidence at the scene of the crime. Yeah so he gouged out her eye with his knife, he stabbed her around four times (still unsure) and slashed her numerous times and then stabbed her in her heart. No evidence was left. No DNA was left, he was in the clear.

The Clydebank Post ran a small, but well written, story about the crime, saying that the police had been called on the 21st and declared that the body had been there for around 48 hours. (Does no one use that lane anymore?) The newspaper reported that the police are appealing for witnesses or any information, but feel it was a robbery gone wrong.

He smiled at that, but what was worrying him was the fact that he was still feeling as though he could do this again. If he couldn't just steal money – he could kill for money! He felt far superior to the law, almost above them. Higher than anyone else. But then some days tears would run cold down his face and he would start wondering why he got out of bed at all. He remembered one moment he looked out the window and he could see it all. It was blown gales outside, pouring from the sky, but all he saw instead of rain was blood. It was raining blood, small rivers formed – running down the roads into the stanks, blood spatter all over his windows. On one side of the road he saw bodies lying down, blood pouring fast and furious from them. He smiled.

He stood up and turned on the television. *Ah good old freeview!* he thought to himself. He got a freeview box by breaking into a flat just down the road from him, at Clydebank East. It was a high rise flat called Howcraigs Court. He remembered the floor he went to and the flat number – 12d. All he did was kick the door once and it burst open. It looked like someone was just moving in: apart from a bed (tacky looking thing, £69 out of Bed Shed) there was a carpet and TV stand but no TV and a freeview box. He grabbed the freeview box, checked the other rooms: a bathroom (half arsed decorated), the bedroom (no carpet, no decoration), the kitchen (nothing in it at all) and then the living room (some sort of fudge coloured wallpaper). *More like shit stained wallpaper*, he thought. There was a tatty old navy blue leather three seater couch and nothing else, so either the person moving in was poor and didn't have money or had moved out and left that shit behind. He left and was met on the landing by a couple of young teenage lads. "Where you been mate?"

He looked them each in the eye. "12d is empty, and some stuff in there worth taken. I've already caved in the door."

The boys laughed. "Cheers mate," and headed off towards the broken into flat.

Now he tuned to channel 86 (Babestation) pulled down his trousers and boxers and grabbing a dirty towel, he sat on his cheap ass couch and watched the gorgeous blonde babe with big tits writhing about on the large silk covered bed. He grabbed hold of his cock and began stroking it up and down. His member got hard and started pulsing. He knew it wouldn't be long until he exploded. He smirked. "Come on you dirty slut – I know you want my cock deep in your mouth. Make me cum Leah (the babe on the channel), make me cum all over your big tits!" He felt his ball sacks tighten and then seconds later he squirted everywhere. White gloopy man juice shot out of his member, some shooting as high as the ceiling, the rest (nearly) hitting him square in the face. He sat back, exhausted, still stroking his manhood. That was his exercise for the day.

Trousers up, telly off, and now to score some drugs; but firstly money was needed. So he pulled on his jacket, grabbed his knife, placed it into his jacket pocket and left for the day. He knew if push came to shove the knife was there to be used, but deep down he didn't want to/have to use it. All he needed was his drugs, and all because his mother made him this way.

Door slammed and locked - he was on his way.

9
Crime Doesn't Pay
25th January 2000

William Light sat at his desk in the police station contemplating on what to write on his report - he had just arrested a few teenagers for breaking and entering into a flat on a very troubled housing estate. The boys gave him and the attending officer grief: shouting, swearing, lashing out at them until both William and the other officer man-handled them and pushed them to the ground, restraining them and then handcuffing them.

"You gotta believe us ya dick, we didn't break into the flat, we just entered and took the stuff. The flat seemed empty. We met a guy on the landing; he broke in and told us about the other stuff in it!"

William nodded. "Well you are both under arrest for burglary; maybe not house breaking but burglary none-the-less!"

"Come on mate, look the guy nicked a freeview box!" the younger of the two stated.

The officer pinning him down looked at William then back

down the teen, "What did he look like then?" He picked the teen up so he was at a standing position.

"Yer Maw!" he spat in his face and then laughed.

Both William and the officer marched them to the van.

"Come on officer – please don't arrest us, well me anyway, my maw will kill me!" the youngest one said.

"Does this look like a face that is bothered son?" William responded. At the van, he opened the back door followed by the gate and literally threw the teens in. Youngest followed by the oldest.

Now he was sitting at his desk, writing the report out. He already got the council out to the flat to board up the front door and pin a note to the door which stated, *Please call into Clydebank Police Station as soon as possible*. But no one had came to speak to him, or any other officer - the conclusion was that the house was now empty. The council stated they couldn't get a hold of the owner and didn't know where he was residing now.

So he wrote up the report on the house break and filed it. Just as he was placing it into the filing cabinet the Chief shouted out from his office.

"Guys – we've just had a call come through. A drive off at the BP petrol station at Clydebank East. Who wants it?"

William nodded. "I'll take it sir." He stood up, another exciting day in the Strathclyde police force. One murder, and then back to the same old shit day in day out: drugs, alcohol and theft of petrol. Another officer by the name of Frank Nelson joined him for this one as they both climbed in the patrol car.

10
The Theft, No Problem
25th January 2000

Shoplifting (also known as boosting, five-finger discount, or shrinkage within the retail industry) is theft of goods from a retail establishment. It is one of the most common crimes.

He entered the shop and started walking up the aisle, browsing just like any other customer. He noticed that security was away on their break and that there were basically only three staff members on today: one on the till, one in the back warehouse and one in the milk aisle. Grabbing a few packets of pre-packed meat, he placed them inside his jacket. It was annoying him that he had to do this, but living on Jobseeker's Allowance was pitiful. it didn't cover what he needed on a day to day basis. (Thanks obviously to his dear old mum, who by all accounts will be his victim soon!) He figured he could sell the meat at the pub or around the neighbourhood doors and be able to get money for some blues or anything to take the pain away.

After walking round the aisle, he noticed that he was being watched by the staff member from the till, who gave three short blasts on a bell. *To signify a shoplifter on premises perhaps?* He began to get sweaty and started walking fast; he looked over his shoulder and saw the white shirt with the stiff black tie, the black straight trousers and the blue SIA badge swinging around his neck coming towards him. The guy was an old-timer, roughly fifty-five, he thought.

"Oi you stop right there!" the old timer shouted.

He just looked at him and smirked, he neared the shop entrance and the security officer caught up with him placing a hand directly on his shoulder. "I told you to stop!"

He spun round and faced the security officer, cocked his head to one side and produced the knife. "Try that again dick!" he grunted.

The old timer let go of his shoulder and stood back. "OK son, no need for the knife, just give me back the stock and we will call it quits?"

He just smirked at him. "Get to fuck arsehole!" He swiped the blade at the officer, who jumped back and fell into a display of canned beans. He just smiled at the old guy and ran out the shop.

The security officer got back up and grabbed his phone. He punched in 999. "Police please I want to report a shoplifter!" The officer walked out the door and glanced up and down the street but couldn't see the shoplifter anywhere. "Hi police, yes I want to report a shoplifter. My name is James Sinclair; I'm security at the Lidl store in Clydebank Retail Park."

The operator was taking notes of this. "And do you have the offender on premises?"

James went back into the store bowing his head and was met by the staff: two guys and one girl. He shook his head. "No sorry, he got away."

There was a long pause. "Can you describe the offender?"

James nodded and cleared his throat. "Yes, he was about twenty years old. Was wearing a blue jumper and dark jeans, and had a cream coloured jacket on. It seemed to be covered in what I think was blood, not a lot just a few speckles."

The operator continued noting this down. "Can you describe his appearance?"

James gulped. "Not really, he had his hood up so couldn't see his hair. But he did have stubble and cold blue piercing eyes. He looked – evil!"

"OK," the operator began, "we will send officers to see you. They shouldn't be too long, just hang tight."

On that the old timer hung up the phone.

11
Sorted
25th January 2000

"Whoa that was lucky," he said to himself. He sat in his flat, sweat dripping; he had already sold the meat from Lidl. He got enough money from the old guys in Alexander's pub at Clydebank train station. Then ventured to his dealer and got something for the pain. "Damn you Mum!" he shouted out, grabbing a handful of blues and popping each one right into his mouth. Soon he would be fleeing, but first he had to figure out his plan. His plan to kill his mum.

He knew she ruined him. He knew she would have to pay the price. He knew it would take time. But he had to plan it. Yeah he killed that old bitch in the lane. She shouldn't have starred at him. Police will file it under robbery gone wrong. No prints, no DNA. So he was safe for now. He intended on just killing his mum, but thought if he had done that he would obviously be the prime suspect. Either him, his wee brother or his good old police officer wanker of a dad. But best bet was on him, 1/7 odds on favourite to kill her.

So far newspapers (locally) claimed the killing as robbery

gone wrong. The file was still open none-the-less, but he knew they had nothing on him. He was just another junkie, waiting on his next fix. No hassle to the cops and he knew that good old Lidl had no cameras - *fucking dafties* - so he certainly wasn't going to be identified.

He began feeling really tired, the blues finally kicking in. He lay back on his sofa, closed his eyes and fell asleep.

12
Nightmares
25th January 2000

"Stab her. Rip her tongue out. Cut her throat. Pull out her intestines. Do it Zach. Do it for us. If not, do it for yourself!"

The voices screamed at him. The dark figure deep inside his mind, urged him to carry out the evil deeds.

"Who are you? What do you want?" he screamed.

"Do it Zach – make her pay. She abused you and now abuses your brother! He hates life there. You should have taken him with you!" it screamed at him. It was such an earth shattering scream that he had to place his hands over his ears.

"I asked him. Didn't I? I asked him to come with me, he said no. He wanted to stay with the cow! Not my fault. Not my fault. Not my fault."

"Zach you have turned into a monster. You have killed once. You covered your tracks. Kill more and then get your mum!" it told him.

He nodded to the figure. "OK I will do it!"

His eyes shot open, sweat pouring down him, smelling like vinegar. Time for another murder!

He smiled.

13
No Idea
January 25th 2000

"So what you are saying Mr Sinclair, is that this store has no CCTV? No alarm system at front of store? And no tagging on various products in here?" William Light asked.

The Security Officer nodded, disgracefully.

"So how do you expect us to deal with this shoplifter then?"

The old timer looked at William. "I have a pretty good description of him, if that helps?"

The other officer looked up from his notebook and glared at the security officer. "Mr Sinclair – do you want us to put wanted posters up or something? This isn't the bloody wild west, it's Clydebank!"

The old timer looked away. "Well I just thought-"

William cut him off. "You thought nothing." They were joined by the Lidl manager, a cocky little 20-something. William turned to him. "So you're the manager then?"

The kid nodded.

"We can't do anything here. No CCTV, no alarm activation, no nothing. What we suggest is you get those things in to stop this this happening anymore. But I would get it in fast, cause as soon as word hits the street that this store has no security apart from him" he pointed to the old timer, "then you will get done over constantly."

The manager nodded and then the officers left.

Outside they walked over to the car park towards their car. "Fucking retail security firms these days. Hire old timers that can't do their job properly. I fucking hate them."

14
Hello Bitch, Goodbye Bitch
26th January 2000

It had just turned midnight: a new day, a new dawn, a new kill. Wednesday – some say the middle of the week, he thought it was a death day. Another day to kill.

He walked along past the Clydebank bus stance, along past the bus shelters and crossed the road next to the corner shop. As he passed by the fish and chip shop, there she was.

Her short black dress and her black high heels: the perfect candidate, the perfect kill. He pulled up his black hood and walked towards her.

She had just stumbled out of the local pub known as John Browns by herself. *Good.* She began walking past Tote the bookmakers and headed left under the bridge and then right past the lawyers office towards Dalmuir. He walked behind her, tailing her: not getting too close and not getting too far behind.

As she passed by The Wee Loan Company, building, he made his move. He checked his location – *good no one in sight*. He moved up behind her and grabbed her, pulling her while she tried kicking and screaming down the lane beside the building. He spun her around and slapped her across the face, making her fall to the grime infested ground. He cocked his head to one side and heard them again.

"Kill her, don't let her live."

He shook his head and pulled out his knife. The girl just screamed and tried to get back to her feet. She kneeled and he struck her on her head, causing her to fall and strike her head on the rough textured wall. Her head scraped down it and she slumped back to the ground. She tried to get back up, but considered crawling instead. She crawled through the rubbish. *(What did you think it was going to be clean!?)* He followed her slowly and then struck.

The knife swung back and forth across the girl's back forming a criss-cross pattern. She screamed and screamed as blood poured from her wounds.

He smiled.

He continued sticking her with the knife. She continued screaming, but no-one came. She turned over onto her back and stared up at her killer. He stood over her, but replaced the knife back in his pocket. He noticed a Buckfast bottle lying against the wall, bent down and picked it up. He smiled. "Ah good old fuckfast!" He hit the bottle against the wall: once, twice and then it smashed leaving a jagged edge. Without hesitation he stuck the bottle into her throat. Blood spurted out through the bottle. Her hands went straight to the throat.

He smiled. "Are you happy now?"

From the distance he heard the voices. "Yessssssssssssss.

Second murder – for fun.

15
Talking to Himself
26th January 2000

He starred into the mirror above the bathroom sink. Asking himself if there was anybody out there. No voices spoke to him. He was all alone. He couldn't get help, who was he going to go to – the police? *Please*. What would he say? 'I hear voices in my head and kill for them, but really I'm on a path to kill my parents. Firstly my mum because she abused me, got me hooked on drugs and then my dad because he left me and my brother!'

Yeah that'll go down like a lead balloon. He shook his head, raised his fist and smashed the mirror. He put both hands up to his temples and screamed. He turned, went into the living room and switched on the television. He sat down and clicked to STV, the news was on and low and behold there was Clydebank; for the first time in so many years, Clydebank was on the regional news!

He turned up the volume and listened to the reporter.

"We are now going live to the town of Clydebank where Angus McDermott is reporting on a vicious brutal murder that has taken place. Angus can you hear me?" the newsreader stated.

The reporter, Angus McDermott, nodded. "Yes John I can. I am live in Clydebank, the town made famous by the John Brown's Shipyard, where the likes of the QE2 was built. Today we report on a murder of a young woman, struck down before she even turned twenty-one. Viciously stabbed to death and left dead in an alleyway for the world to see. I have Chief Inspector Alex Grimm with me from the Clydebank division of Strathclyde police. Chief Inspector, can you enlighten the public about what happened here?"

A man, roughly fifty years of age, stood in a black suit and tie with the reporter. "Well, at 0900 hours this morning, Clydebank police got a call to attend here with the view that a body was found with multiple stab wounds. On arrival we discovered that a young woman of twenty years of age was murdered, most likely with a knife and then a broken bottle. We have informed the family of the woman and will not release her name until the family tell us so."

"Has this murder been linked to the murder of the elderly woman who was struck down the same way Chief?"

The Inspector sighed. "The elderly woman in question died this month, also in the Clydebank area, but is not yet linked with this case. We are treating both murders as separate cases."

"But Inspector, the elderly woman in question was also stabbed to death wasn't she?"

Yet again the Inspector sighed. "I am sorry, no more questions. We will update as soon as we know." He walked away from the reporter.

"Well John that's the story from this side of the tracks, now back to the studio."

He leaned back with his hands behind his head and smiled. Another murder and the police are not linking them together. First murder, you could say for money, but deep down it was because the old bitch starred at him the wrong way. The second murder was just because the voices told him too. Or it was to get closer to his father. He knew his father was living, or at least working, in this shitty town and he would find him.

Eventually.

16
A Grave Mistake
29th January 2000

Andrew stood in the back garden in the pouring rain: standing in the mud, digging a big hole in the ground. He kept looking down. "Not another peep Mum, time to go to sleep!"

He shovelled more dirt into the hole, covering the nasty thing in the hole.

Pouring more dirt into the hole, Andrew sang his little song to his hidden treasure again. "Not another peep, time to go to sleep."

Andrew glared down, watching his mother twitch as the dirt piled on top of her.

"Now it doesn't feel like the world's on my shoulders, you're gone Mum. It's over," Andrew sang.

If only it was real…

Andrew jumped up into a sitting position in his bed. Just a dream, a vivid one at that. Andrew wished it was real.

Could he kill his own mum?

And get away with it?

He shook his head. *Not a chance in hell!* Then his dear old mother shouted, "Andrew come in here, you know what time it is."

Andrew sighed and mumbled, "Round fucking twenty-five of 'yes mum I'll do that to you' and 'yes mum just sit on me and do what you want to me'. I have to find Zach or my dad; it's the only way to stop this. Once and for all!"

Andrew climbed out of bed and made his way to his loving mum's bedroom once again. He opened the door, walked in slowly and closed the door behind him.

17
No Further Forward
1st February 2000

William Light sat across from the Chief of police. "So what do we do?"

"To be perfectly honest with you mate, I ain't got a clue!" Alex began. "No clues, no fingerprints. But let's just be grateful that we only have two bodies, two unsolved murders."

"Yeah that we know about!" William replied.

"William, what do you want me to do?" Alex struck back. "Do you want me to get the whole of Clydebank police force out and about looking for bodies? Missing people? Things like that? That's a lot of time and money and patience."

"I'm just saying Alex," William began, "we have had two murders in exactly the same month, two bodies cut to shreds and brutally slain in our backyard so to speak. I do think it's the work of the same person, and-,"

He was cut short. "William, we have no evidence to prove the cases are linked, we just have to wait and see."

"Wait and see!?" William frowned back. He stood up and moved to the window overlooking the Clydebank retail park.

He turned back towards the Chief and long time friend of his. "Wait and see for what exactly?"

"If this person or persons strike again," Alex answered. "We can't rule out that it isn't connected."

"And we can't rule out that it is!" William responded. "Alex, mate, seriously we can't just sit back and wait, the public are scared, hell I'm scared!"

"William, do I have to remind you that I'm the Chief here, not you. So if I tell you we wait, we wait. And anyway if it is the same killer, then he will strike again, I have employed undercover officers to stake out the areas in and around where the bodies were found. Now only I and you know this, so don't go blabbing to the newspapers or someone else – OK?"

William nodded. "At least that is something I suppose." He made his way to the office door.

"Oh, and William?" Alex said. William turned. "Keep in mind that if it is the same killer, and if he truly wants to be a serial killer, he has to notch up a few more than two. But I – we - won't let it get that far – will we?"

William shook his head and then left the office.

But the devil had descended on the small town of Clydebank, and not just Alex and William knew this.

Darkness had fallen on Clydebank, but the Light had been

resurrected and the Light will shine on the town and cause chaos, like nothing before.

It was only a matter of time.

D. P. Sloan

18
The Suicide Helper
21st July 2000

He watched as the man clambered up over the railings and clung onto the pole. The drop to the River Clyde below was around one hundred feet. The Erksine Bridge was the venue the man picked to end his life. He smirked at he thought of the man taking the coward's way out - suicide was for the weak - but he had a plan to stop him jumping.

It had been over five months since he killed the girl. He thought there was no need to kill again at the moment, he didn't want the police looking directly into the murders. So he took a break, so to speak.

Now he watched him from across the bridge. Watched him as he stumbled onto the railings. He was trying to figure out: should he help him, or just let him jump.

It was a long way down off the top of the Erskine Bridge. The Erskine Bridge is a cable-stayed box girder bridge spanning the River Clyde in west central Scotland, connecting West Dunbartonshire with Renfrewshire.

He watched as the man clambered up over the supposedly

safety railings and stood teetering on the edge. Cars drove passed but didn't slow down: either they didn't notice him or just couldn't be bothered.

He made his way across the road when it was clear and stood just to the back of the man. The man didn't notice him. The man was dressed in all black. A black hooded top, black cargo pants, black boots.

"Hi," he said.

The man turned his head round.

"Can I help you? Do you need help? My name is Zach, Zach Light. What's yours?"

The suicidal man looked down at this other man. "Go to fuck. Leave me alone."

"Listen," he said to him. "I've been there – here myself, I'm just offering you a helping hand, a hand not to do it. A hand so to speak to help you."

"And how do you plan on doing that?" the man asked him. He gripped tightly onto the metal pole.

"Cause I know what you did and I'm willing to help you and keep your secret," he answered. He moved a step closer to the railing.

The man looked down at him with a puzzled look on his face. "You know what I did!? I didn't do anything! I just want to end my life!"

"So you didn't kill your wife, her lover and his son with a kitchen knife?"

The man loosened his grip on the pole and began coming down off the railings, "H – how did you know that?"

"As I said," he began, "I've been watching you. Now get back on safe ground and tell me your name."

The man came down completely off the large scary structure and stood face to face with his new friend as such. "My name is Kane, Jacob Kane."

"Well Jacob, as I said before, my name is Zach Light and we have business to discuss," he told the troubled man.

"What kind of business?" Jacob asked him.

He smiled. "I can help you, if you help me!" He extended his hand and Jacob shook it. "Let's go back to my house and we can discuss my business plan."

Jacob nodded. He didn't know he was making a deal with the devil himself.

19
Jacob Kane
12th February 2000

"Shut the fuck up bitch and sit down!" Jacob screamed at his wife.

She sat there crying as he stood above her. "OK," his young wife Sally replied.

They had been married for six years now and had a two year old daughter named Rebecca. Jacob worked nightshift to put more money in the house, but tonight he wasn't feeling too good and his boss sent him home, only for him to discover his wife in bed with another man. His daughter sleeping in her bed, while they had sex in their bed.

"If Rebecca wakes up, I swear I'll kill you! What am I saying I am going to kill you, and Rebecca doesn't need to see what I'm about to do," Jacob yelled. "Stop crying you slut. How could you? How could you do this to me? Oh what's the matter, you scared?"

Sally shook nervously and tears streamed down her face.

"Too bad bitch," Jacob began, "you caused this, why did you do this to me? Look what you've made me do!" he pointed to the man lying on the floor, "He won't be going to work tomorrow will he? Everything in this house is mine!" Jacob paced back and forward swinging the knife in his hand. "How could you let him sleep in our bed? Look at him Sally; look at your boyfriend now!"

"No!" Sally screamed.

"I said look at him!" Jacob yelled back. "He ain't so hot now is he? Little cunt." He knelt over the man's body.

"Why you doing this?" Sally asked.

"Shut the fuck up!" Jacob responded while turning the body over.

Sally cried, "You're never going to get away with this!"

"I don't give two fucks!" came Jacobs's response. "Come on, let's go out for a while." Jacob pulled at her arm.

"No!" Sally yelled again, trying desperately to stop him pulling at her.

Jacob managed to get her to her feet and pulled her out of the house to the driveway. "Get in!"

"We can't leave Rebecca, what if she wakes up?" Sally questioned.

Jacob smiled a cruel smile as he pushed his wife into the passenger seat. "Don't worry I'll be right back, but you won't!"

Go to Sleep

A worried and a shocked look came over Sally. Her time was up surely, or was her husband, the man she had loved for over six years just joking? She knew this was no joke – he had already killed her lover and her lover's son, who was watching TV when he came back into the house to discover them 'at it'. She knew Jacob had a bad, almost evil, streak but thought he wouldn't be capable of doing a thing like this.

Two bodies down and only her to go.

Jacob climbed into the driver's seat and locked the doors, he started up his Megane and squealed away down the road, "I can't believe you did this, you bitch. I mean me cheating on you when I was eighteen, I could understand but now, with us being married and having Rebecca. Why? How could you?!"

"I love you," Sally declared, clearing the salty tears from her cheeks.

"Oh God my brain is racing." Jacob yelled. He shot a hand up to his temple. "You think this is a joke?"

"No," Sally cried.

"Exactly, there's a four year old boy dead with a slit throat in our living room. Ha-ha, oh well at least he's next to his daddy now!" Jacob turned and yelled at her. "You loved him didn't you?"

"No!" Sally stammered.

"Lies Sally, stop telling me lies! What don't you love me anymore? Do you think I'm ugly now?"

Sally shook her head, "No, it's not that."

"No, you think I'm ugly," Jacob responded.

"Baby," Sally cried, she reached a hand over to him.

"Get the fuck away from me; don't touch me," Jacob screamed. "I HATE YOU! I HATE YOU! I SWEAR TO GOD I HATE YOU! OH MY GOD I LOVE YOU! How the fuck could you do this to me?"

"I'm sorry," Sally declared.

"How the fuck could you do this to me?" Jacob yelled. He floored the accelerator and the car sped up along the road.

Fifteen minutes later they were parked up on the dirt road leading to Kilpatrick hills. Hills set in history, made famous by the Romans who built the Antonine wall.

"Come on get out," Jacob screamed at his terrified wife.

"No, I'm scared," Sally relayed back to him.

Jacob opened up the driver's door, raced round and pulled the passenger door open with a hard yank. "I said get out bitch!" he grabbed hold of her hair and pulled.

"Let go of my hair," Sally sobbed. "Ow, you're hurting me. Look we can just pack up everything and take Rebecca and leave town."

"Fuck you," Jacob screamed. "The only place you are going is six feet under. Do you understand?"

"I'm so sorry," Sally sobbed again.

"I've came up with the perfect story you see," Jacob began, "you and your lover are arguing and you have enough hell we all know what kind of temper you have, don't we? You run into the kitchen and grab a knife, he comes in and you both struggle and in the midst of it all you slash his throat. Then his son walks in crying cause he can't sleep and you kill him and just so you feel some remorse you end your own life."

He was cut off as his petrified wife made a run for it, but tripped. Jacob caught up with her and pulled her up, "You were supposed to love me in sickness and in health and until death do us part, those vows we took. Hell you were probably fucking anything that walks!" Jacob raised the knife and sliced his scared wife across the throat, she scratched and clawed at her throat before falling down dead.

"NOW ROT IN THE DIRT BITCH, BLEED AND ROT!" Jacob spat at his dying wife.

A few minutes later Sally fell to the ground – dead. Now Jacobs's task was to get her home and clean up any evidence that he was there. He carried his wife back to the car, and dumping her in the trunk he then climbed into his car and drove back home.

Standing just off too the left in the thick overgrowth was Zach Light. He liked what he saw.

Twenty minutes later Jacob pulled into his driveway in Bowling - a quiet neighbourhood where no neighbours interfered at all with each other's problems, it had a population of around 500 people.

It was the dead of night and Jacob carried his dead wife into the house. He placed her down in the living room, next to her dead lover's body and that of her lover's son. It was time to clear up his 'evidence' he then went back to the car and drove away back down the road. He pulled over to the side just north of the Kilpatrick roundabout.

He picked up his mobile phone and dialled his boss; it rang for a few seconds and then was answered. "Hi John, it's Jacob. I was wondering if I could come back in? - Yeah I know I wasn't feeling right but it turned out, it was just indigestion. Cool, I'll be about ten minutes. No I didn't get home, got to the garage, got a bite to eat and a coffee then felt good. OK see you soon, bye."

Jacob smiled; no one would (hopefully) suspect a thing. He would get the call in the early hours of the morning (he guessed) from the police explaining what happened. And if they questioned or suspected him then he would have witnesses, because he did go to the garage and he did have a receipt for the food he bought, but the garage that he went too didn't have CCTV so they wouldn't be able to trace his exact movements.

Jacob Kane would get away with it, no one knew.

Except one person did know - and he was watching Jacob's every move.

20
A Simple Police Matter
13th February 2000

"Hello 999, what is your emergency?"

"Please help! I've just came home from work, my house is trashed and my wife, a man and boy I don't know have been killed. Please send help!" Jacob Kane sobbed down the phone.

"Sir please calm down, can you tell me where you are?" the operator asked.

"It's…its…" Jacob began, "566 Lewis Crescent, Bowling. Please hurry, there's so much blood."

"Emergency services are on their way sir," the operator began, "please leave the house and wait outside. Sir, can you tell me your name please?"

"It's Jacob, Jacob Kane," Jacob sobbed down the phone.

"OK Mr Kane," the operator assured him, "stay calm, vacate the premises and wait outside. The police will be with you shortly."

Jacob hung up and smiled a bit, then got back into character and brought the tears on again. He knew his baby girl was lying sleeping in the bedroom down the hall, but he had to act distressed and 'out of it' until the police came then he was going to use the wild card.

He exited the house of death and sat outside on the grass, waiting for the emergency services to arrive. He knew once the sirens came tearing down the road, the neighbours would come out for a sneaky peek.

It was within a few minutes (literally) that the place was swarming with blue flashing lights: police cars and ambulances. Two officers walked over to Jacob, who still remained seated on the damp winter grass.

"Are you Jacob Kane?" the younger officer of the two asked him.

Jacob nodded and stood up. "Yes, please help her, I – I can't go back in there. My beautiful wife…"

"It's OK sir," began the slightly older looking officer, "you come with me."He turned to the younger officer. "You got this Jason?"

The young officer, Jason, nodded and the older officer guided Jacob away to the police car.

A good crowd had turned out to watch this episode of *Brit Cops* in action.

Officer Jason turned and walked into the newly named crime scene, on entering he was met with the trashed living room and three bodies on the floor. He checked for pulses on all the victims, but all victims were dead.

He tried to dodge the blood spatter everywhere as he began to leave the house. Just as he neared the front door, he heard a soft cry. He turned, trying to focus on where it was coming from. He heard it again, puzzled, he began to move towards the sound and then he heard from outside the house. "Oh my God, my baby! My baby Rebecca is in there!"

The officer turned and looked out into the street, Jacob Kane was being held back by his partner, he saw Jacob crying and then collapse to the ground.

The officer turned and made his way down the hallway, following the sound of the baby's cry. He got to the bedroom where the noise was coming from and saw a beautiful baby girl lying in bed. He picked her up and moved back through the house and out into the street.

Jacob looked up. "Rebecca! Oh my God thank you, thank you. Is she OK officer?"

Officer Jason gave the baby a once over. "She's fine, just needs her daddy. You OK to hold her?"

Jacob nodded and smiled.

"Listen Mr Kane, we will need to take a statement from you about tonight, are you OK to do that?"

Jacob sniffled and nodded. "Can you take Rebecca to my mum's house? Then I'll answer any questions you want officer."

The older officer of the two chimed in, "Sure I'll do that, what's your mum's address?"

Jacob gave him the address and the officer wrote it down. He then took the baby over to his car.

Jacob turned to the other officer. "Are they all dead?"

The officer nodded. "Unfortunately – yes I'm afraid."

Jacob shook his head. "No, no, no, please no!"

"Mr Kane, are you sure you'll be OK answering questions?" the officer said while trying to comfort him.

Jacob nodded. "Where do you want to go?"

"We will go down to the station and take your statement, away from prying eyes if that's OK?" the officer asked.

Jacob nodded. "What about my house?"

"An officer will guard it, and once forensics have finished we will lock it up until it's safe for you to return," the young man reassured him.

"OK," Jacob agreed.

With that, they both turned and walked to the awaiting police car. Once in they drove to the police station.

From the crowd Zach Light watched and smiled, he wanted

to give the man a round of applause for his great acting.

Their paths would soon cross for the worse.

21
The Voice
15th August 2000

He lay there listening to it. The voice telling him what he was to do. He called it a 'HE' but in reality it was a cluster of voices.

He listened as it told him what 'HE' wanted to do, and in all fairness what 'HE' wanted him to do.

"Climb up to the window, look at her then climb in and slowly shatter her brain matter and batter her with a bat, as a matter of fact that will splatter her. Tell her, I'm your secret admirer, I'm back to ravish you. Believe me she will put up a fight, she will be strong. But just tell her, you're no match for Dracula. Now Zach prolong her plight, and then go back to stabbing her, dismember her limbs, simple as that, cadaver her. Now the new bit - take your 'subject' Jacob with you, make sure he has his camcorder now, and now tell him to zoom in with the lens, then pan back the camera. Now stand back, and marvel at your work Zach, because after all you are the modern day Jack the Ripper."

He sat there as the voice disappeared. He nodded and

thought to himself, *what better way to continue his path of destruction, the destruction leading directly to the two people that literally has caused this?* His victims, the old lady and the young twenty-something girl. His dad and mum caused this and they will pay in due course, but for now as his little voice in his head said again, "Let's have some fun!"

"Hey Jacob?" he shouted.

"Don't call me that," came the voice from the bedroom. "My name is Kane! Call me Kane!"

"All right all right," he yelled back. "Kane fancy doing that favour I asked?"

22
The Statement
13th February 2000

"Interview with Mr Jacob Francis Kane at 0900 hours, interview conducted by myself PC Jason Barr, alongside Police Officer William Light. Mr Kane, for the tape can you say your full name, date of birth and your address please," Officer Barr said.

The interview room was like a cell: grey-blue walls, an old tatty table and three chairs. One for Jacob and across from him the other two where both officers had sat, listening to Jacob state his name.

Jacob sat back and the sweat started dripping slowly off of him. He started twiddling his thumbs.

"Are you OK Jacob?" stated Officer Light.

"Yeah," Jacob began, "Just shocked that's all. I mean you don't expect to finish work and come back to utter carnage!"

"Mr Kane, can you confirm where you were last night leading into today?" Officer Barr asked.

Without hesitation Jacob answered. "I was at work, I work nightshift at the Clydebank Asda. I started at 9 p.m. but around

10 p.m. I wasn't feeling too good. So my duty manager, John Flannigan, said I could go home."

"And did you go home?" Officer Light asked. He was writing down notes while his fellow officer kept looking at Jacob.

"I got in my car and started driving back home, but I stopped at the garage as I thought I was going to be sick. My stomach was turning over and over. So I rushed into the garage and asked to use the toilet. The assistant gave me the key and I went in. Thankfully I wasn't sick; I just needed to release some gas!" Jacob explained.

"What happened next?" the young officer asked, while shifting his body weight in the tatty old chair.

"I gave the girl the key back, bought a few things and left." Jacob answered. "I was feeling much better and-"

"What did you buy Mr Kane?" Officer Light asked, cutting him off.

"I bought a bacon and cheese turnover and a large coffee," Jacob answered, "Why do you ask that, when I gave you receipt anyway?"

"Just checking," stated Officer Light.

"Do you think I'm lying or something?" Jacob queried.

"Not at all Mr Kane, we just have to go through this with

every witness or suspect," Officer Barr replied. "So after the garage where did you go next?"

"Well I began driving back home, but then pulled over just at Kilpatrick roundabout, you know the one where it cuts off to Erskine Ferry Road?" Jacob answered.

Both officers nodded in unison.

"Please continue," Officer Light stated.

"Well I pulled over and drank my coffee and ate my turnover, I was feeling much better, so I waited there and closed my eyes for a bit, then phoned my boss up and asked if I could come back into work, I told him that it was just a bit of indigestion," Jacob stated.

"We talked to your boss and just for the record, his version matches yours," Officer Barr stated.

Jacob shifted his weight in the chair. "When I finished work in the morning, I turned up to my house to find, find…well you know!" He bowed his head and started crying.

Officer Light turned off the recorder and stood up. He made his way round to Jacob and put a hand around his shoulder. "Mr Kane, we will get whoever did this to your wife, we will do our hardest to catch the murderer."

Jacob lifted his head. "Officer, who were the man and the child? The ones who were dead alongside my wife in the living room?"

"Mr Kane," Officer Light began, "we can't release that information now. But as soon as we know who they are, or why they were in there with your wife, we will tell you."

Jacob nodded and wiped away his tears. "Can I go now?"

Officer Light nodded. "Yes you can, although you can't go back to your house at the moment as it's a crime scene. Can you stay at your mother's?"

Jacob nodded and stood up. He thanked the officers and left the interview room. William Light closed the door and turned and faced the other officer. "So what do you think?"

"I don't know Billy; there is something about this that I'm not really sure about!" Jason answered. He stood up, ejected the tape and grabbed hold of all their notes. He walked over to William. "I just don't know mate, still seems fishy!"

With that they both left the room and made their way to their desks.

Outside Jacob walked away from the Clydebank Police Station and down towards the Clydebank Shopping Centre. He wiped tears away from his eyes, but at the same time he smiled.

He had just got away with murder.

23
Three and Easy
16th August 2000

"Right you just gotta come into the room with the camcorder as soon as I say so and I'll do the rest –OK?" He told Kane.

Kane nodded but screwed his face up. "And the reason you are doing this again is…?"

"Because I want too," he shot back. "In this day and age, you don't need a reason to do anything. Don't worry, all you're going to do is record it; I'll do the hard work."

"Before we go in," Kane began, "this is the only time you've done this isn't?"

He smirked at him. "Kane of course it is!" he lied. "I saw what you done to that bitch of a wife of yours and thought if you can get away with murder – literally - then I should give it a try – that's all!"

"But why the camcorder?" Kane asked.

He began steadying the ladder against the window. "For my pleasure later on!" he smiled.

Kane shrugged his shoulders and nodded. Kane watched as his new friend (almost a saviour in his eyes) climbed the ladder to the opened bedroom window. (Security not in Clydebank houses I'm afraid!) As he got to the top of the ladder he slowly crept in and over the windowsill. Kane began climbing the ladder, watching around him for any movement of people or animals. No one was insight. He clambered up the rungs and quietly entered the bedroom. He saw his friend standing above the bed where a pretty young girl lay - not much older than seventeen.

"Kane start recording now," he whispered as he produced the knife and the small wooden bat. He turned back to the young teenage girl. "Hey baby, waken up," he whispered in her ear.

She stirred a bit, but didn't wake up.

"Hey honey, wakey, wakey," he whispered again. This time the pretty girl started to open her eyes and while trying to adjust to the darkness, she saw the two shadows: one leaning over her and the other standing at the foot of the bed holding something which flashed a red dot now and again.

"Who – who are you?" She sat up quickly, startled more than anything. She pulled the quilt cover up to her chin covering the pink vest top that covered her young breasts.

"Don't panic, I'm not going to do anything." He reassured her. "I've noticed you about the place and didn't have the guts to tell you how beautiful you were."

"What?" she began. "So...so you think you can just sneak into my bedroom in the middle of the night to pay me a compliment?" She curled up against the wall, trying to get as far away from the two strangers as you could.

"You can call me a stalker if you want," he whispered, "but I just had to see you. I had to tell you how much this here means to me – to us!"

"So what does this mean to you then?" she asked. She was becoming increasingly worried about what was going to happen, there was a young man wearing a black hooded top standing above her and she knew there was another person in the darkness at the foot of her bed with what appeared to be a camcorder.

"It means more to me than it means to you," he told her as he pulled the wooden bat into view.

Her eyes went wide with fright and she was just about to scream when he raised the bat and brought it forcefully down on the young teenager's skull. Once, twice, three times the bat struck the bone, and after the third hit a 'crack' noise followed by a 'pop' noise resulting in the girl's body becoming limp. He swung the bat down again and again, and every time he raised the bat Kane with his camcorder picked up the blood and hair clinging to it.

"Kane zoom in," he told his partner.

Kane obliged, catching the image in the viewfinder. At first Kane felt sick, but that disappeared - he did murder three people after all, including a young four year old boy! "Now pan back," Kane heard his friend say. Kane again obliged as he saw his friend put the bat on the bedside cabinet and produce a knife, in silence he watched as his friend began stabbing the girl repeatedly with the knife, his friend looked at him as blood dripped onto the bed sheets and down the teenager's young silky smooth skin. He looked directly at the camcorder, "Guess I am a modern day Jack the Ripper!"

Kane continued filming as his friend took the knife and cut deep into the girl's side. He pulled the skin apart and delved deep into the small of the back and then taking his knife he cut out something that Kane couldn't really see at the angle he was standing in. Kane heard him cut the thing out and he turned towards the camera.

"It's the kidney!" he declared.

"What you planning on doing with that?" Kane whispered.

"You'll see," he began, "now turn that fucking thing off and let's get out of here!"

Kane, yet again, did as he was told and walked towards the window. He looked out. "Coast is clear," Kane told him before climbing over the windowsill and climbing down the ladder. When Kane got to the bottom he waited anxiously for his friend and star of his own torture movie.

He looked down from the window and signalled that he would be one minute. He turned towards the dead girl and produced a small bag from his pocket. He cocked his hooded head from the left to the right and smiled as he placed the bag on the bloodied bed sheets.

"The time has come!" he smirked as he picked up the small wooden bat and placed it into his hooded top pocket and then picked up the kidney and put it straight into the bag, tying it tight and pushing it into his pocket. The knife simply slipped back into his jean pocket. He turned to the windowsill and climbed out and down the ladder, once at the bottom he removed the ladder and both he and Kane walked back the way they came.

They dumped the ladder not that far away in a rubbish skip outside an old house that recently went on fire and continued on their way back to his house.

The game had just begun.

24
The Love Has Gone
14th February 2000

Saint Valentine's Day: a day of love, of sex, of naughtiness all round.

So why did his beloved mother want him instead of a man her own age?

Andrew hated this day with a vengeance. Yes it was the same as every other day and week in this God forsaken house he called home. But deep down he knew it meant the same old same old.

He waited with baited breath on his dear mother shouting for more loving.

He hated her, even more than normal now. All thoughts of a normal loving relationship between a son and his mother had left him.

Hatred filled his heart now, wanting to leave filled his body.

Needing to leave was a must for him, and today was the day. Monday – the start of a new week: he could leave, just walk out the door and not turn around, not look back at the hell house.

But Andrew couldn't do it, he was scared. He didn't know where his older brother Zach stayed, and he certainly didn't know where his coward of a dad stayed now. Andrew called him a coward, in-fact he called both his brother and father cowards, but deep down he was the one that said he was staying, he remembered the conversation he had with his older brother like it just happened yesterday.

Trapped like a caged animal in his own home, pulled out of school without a blink of warning, his dear mum telling school officials that she would home school him.

Did she home school him? No.

He taught himself via the television and the Internet - oh thank God for the Internet! At least his mother done one thing right – paid the bills on time every time so no one would suspect anything.

Websites helped Andrew get smart, but also opened up a whole other world for him to explore, the search engines were just getting better and all you had to do was type in a few words and up came your answers for what you needed.

Andrew sat in front of his PC and typed into Google: *How to murder your mother.*

It took a bit for the search engine to find stuff due to the dial-up connection but when it did finally find stuff, it uncovered

219 million things about how to murder your mother.

Andrew was impressed. He studied a lot into his new found subject and loved the newspaper clippings, especially the one titled:

SON MURDERS MUM BY BATTERING HER REPEATEDLY WITH A SHOVEL.

Andrew read that story over and over again, and knew that would be the best way to do it. Not messy like with a knife, just plain old battering around the head with a plain old shovel.

Andrew remembered watching a classic horror movie from the mid 1960s titled, *Psycho*, in which a son killed his mother and took on her 'personality', but then in the 1980s a sequel was made and it turned out that the mother he poisoned wasn't his real mother, and in *Psycho 2* his real mother turned up, only to lie to him and betray him, so good old Norman Bates bashed the woman over the head with a simple garden shovel, right there in his kitchen while she was about to drink a lovely cup of tea.

Andrew decided that he would continue just as normal, give his dear old pathetic excuse for a mother his undying love, and then when she was either sleeping, knocked out due to the drink or just plain old out of her face, he would whack her across the head with a shovel and then bury her in the back garden.

Case closed. Andrew happy and then he could leave and find his older brother and his dad.

Andrew thought he would be able to forgive his dad, but he would have to take it day by day, once he met up with him again.

Andrew smiled and then heard his mother shout on him: it was time for her Valentine's treat. He came back into reality and knew deep down how revolted he felt; no son should have to go through this.

But unfortunately this was no normal mother.

Andrew stood up and went to her beckoned call. He walked in her bedroom and closed the door behind him.

"Happy Valentine's day Mum!"

25
More Questions
29th April 2000

"Yeah, I know sometimes things may not always make sense to you right now," Kane said into his little buddle of joy. "But hey, what's Daddy always told you? Stiffen up that upper lip. What you crying about? You got me."

He cradled his daughter carefully as she held onto his index finger, making noises that sounded like talking. The toddler shut her eyes, and drifted into a deep, deep sleep. Kane covered her up and walked out of the bedroom, he entered the living room where his mum sat watching her soap operas.

He sat down across from her. "That's her asleep Mum," he told his fifty-five year old mother.

"Good, good – now ssshhh son, I'm trying to watch this!" his widowed mother told him. Her husband - Kane's dad - passed away two years ago to cancer of the stomach. It ate away at his stomach and then his intestines, there was no way to help or save him.

"Mum, I have to tell you something," Kane interrupted again.

"Not now Jacob, please," his mum waved at him.

Kane wanted to tell someone, anyone (apart from the police that is!) of what he done. He thought if he told his mum she would understand. He needed to tell her. "Mum please!"

"Jacob, for the love of God, can't it wait?" his mum said angrily.

Kane stood up. "OK, OK – I'm going out for a bit." He made his way to the front door, pulled on his jacket and was about to open the door when it chapped.

"Can't I get just a moments peace!" declared his mum. Kane opened the door and found standing on the doorstep: two officers that he had dealt with in the past few weeks. Both officers had questioned him and both officers had turned up at the scene of the murder (which he still can't get into because the police won't let him).

"Hello officers, what can I do for you?" Kane asked politely. The volume of the TV went down and he heard footsteps behind him.

"Hi Mr Kane, hello Mrs Kane," the young officer said. "Mr Kane, I was wondering if you could come back down to the station. We have more questions to ask you?"

Kane's mind went into overdrive, thoughts of a lengthy prison sentence popped up, thoughts of the lies he spun to the police, to his mother and thoughts of not being there for Rebecca when she was older.

"Sure. No problem," Kane answered confidently. "Why, what's up?"

"Just more routine questions Mr Kane," the older officer answered.

Kane nodded and followed the officers out to their police car.

"Jacob, what's happened?" his mother shouted from the doorway.

"It's OK Mum," Kane answered, "just go back indoors and watch your programmes and remember about Rebecca."

Mrs Kane nodded and watched as the police car pulled away.

The drive was mostly silent, apart from the police radios going off now and again. The older officer parked the car and they all got out.

"Just follow us Mr Kane," said the older officer – Officer William Light. Kane nodded and done as he was told.

They all entered interview room one and the same procedure followed: the tape recorder, the two officers sitting across from him.

The tape recorder was started and all present said their names and then the questions started again.

"Mr Kane, I'm going to ask a serious of questions and I need you to answer truthfully," Officer Light began. "Is that OK?"

Kane nodded and so the questions began. Kane answered the exact same as before. He didn't miss a beat, didn't mess up. He said exactly what he said before to them back in February after the 'discovery' of his dead wife and of the two males, one being a boy of just four years old.

"Mr Kane," Officer Light began, "we found out some news with regards to your late wife, now this might shake you up a bit, but your wife was having an affair. The man found dead in your house was your wife's lover."

Kane sat back; of course he knew it was her lover. (He wouldn't have killed him after all if it wasn't!) "Wha-what? Are you serious?"

Both officers nodded. "I'm afraid so Mr Kane," the young officer began, "and the young boy was his son. Someone basically broke into your house, ransacked the place. Slit your wife's throat, her lover's and the young boy's throat and for whatever reason left your baby daughter. Do you know anyone – anyone at all, who would do this? It seems by all accounts the person or persons are trying their hardest to frame you for a murder you said you didn't commit!"

Kane sat there shocked (great acting) he shook his head.

"Can't say I do officers. I mean this case has been going on for months now and I'm guessing you don't have any leads?" he questioned them, waiting on the answer that would make him light up inside.

"Well we verified everything that you said before and you came back clean," the older officer stated. "Obviously we found your DNA in your house, but we were going to find that anyway. We just thought we would cover your tracks again. Basically it was to see if you were lying but-" He was stopped short.

"But I passed," Kane butted in. "You thought I was lying and the best way to catch the killer is to try questioning the number one suspect all over again. Well what are you going to do now?"

"I'm sorry Mr Kane, there's nothing we can do," Officer Light explained. "There was no witnesses, and no DNA, so I am afraid to say this but, we have to close the case and mark it as unsolved. We are truly sorry of your lose Mr Kane and hopefully through time, we may come across something, even something minor, that could catch your wife's killer."

Kane stood up. "So that's it then? That's all this crappy Strathclyde police are going to do to seek justice? My wife is still lying on a slab, as you won't release her - I can't even have a funeral for the mother of my child!"

"Mr Kane," the young officer began, "the body will now be released to you and you can have the funeral your wife so rightly deserves."

Kane nodded and moved towards the door. "Listen," Kane began, "thanks for all your help, she's up there with God enjoying her never ending party." He opened the interview door and got one foot out, when one of the officers shouted.

"Oh Mr Kane?"

He turned round. "Yes?"

"What size of boot are you?" Officer Light asked.

"Size 10," Kane answered. "Why do you asked.

"We found a size 10 footprint in the mud leading up to the house," the officer told him.

"And the reason you're telling me this is because…?" Kane asked.

"Cause, your size 10 foot would fit the footprint," Officer Light answered.

Kane walked back over to the officers. "What are you suggesting officers?" Kane quizzed.

"We are not suggesting anything Mr Kane," Jason stated. "Why? Have you got something to tell us?"

Kane shook his head. "I have told you both everything –

back in February and now today. Yes my DNA would be all over the house – that's because I stay there and with regards to the size 10 footprint, I'm not the only person in my neighbourhood to have size 10 feet am I?" Kane was getting angry.

"Of course not Mr Kane," William answered.

Kane back tracked to the door. "Well I'll go now. Oh, and officers, try and find my wife's killer! At least do something right instead of suspecting me all the time, while someone out there loves the fact they have got away with murder!" he opened the door, walked out and banged the door behind him.

"So what do you think now Billy? You think it's him?" Jason asked.

"I would bet my yearly salary on it!" William Light answered, "Let's keep a watchful eye over Mr Kane, shall we?"

Jason smiled and gathered up the documents of the case.

Outside the police station, Kane began to sweat badly; he knew they were onto him. He knew he was going to get caught; he had to find a way out, a way to end this mess. He got back into the car and headed along Second Avenue and down Duntocher Road onto Dumbarton Road. He pulled over just at the bottom of the high rise flats in Dalmuir and cut the engine. He glanced up through the windshield and looking back at him was the huge structure of the Erskine Bridge.

He knew the police would start staking him out: following him everywhere, watching his every move. It was just a matter of time before he snapped and did something. But he couldn't just disappear in a blink of the eye. He had to wait, bury his God forsaken whore of a wife, act like nothing was wrong, then say his goodbyes and end his life.

Patience he needed - and patience he had.

26
The Plan
21st July 2000

As he helped the poor soul down off the railings of the scary structure, they began walking along the pathway, when he stopped. "If you truly want to get rid of yourself, but don't if you know what I mean then we have to do it right. Take off your watch, take out your wallet, and take off your wedding ring and anything else that's sentimental to yourself."

The man called Jacob did as he was told. They moved towards the safety fencing and glared out and over onto the dark water of the River Clyde below them.

"You got to act as though you have killed yourself and believe me, when the police try searching for your body – which they won't - they'll simply say that the Clyde has claimed another." He told his new found friend. "I'm going to help you and you're going to help me. I know what you did and all I ask in return is you help me just for a bit."

Jacob nodded. "What about my daughter? Will she cope?"

He turned to face him. "Jacob – you did say your goodbyes didn't you?"

Jacob nodded.

"You left a letter? A note of some sort?"

"Yeah," Jacob began. "I put my daughter in her bed and left a letter tucked underneath her. My mum should find it soon."

"Then all is fine then," he told him smiling. He took the items of sentimental value off him and placed them at the foot of the railings. "Now Jacob, listen to me, go down to the Forth and Clyde Canal just east of Dalmuir as if you are heading towards Clydebank shopping centre, I'll meet you there in about an hour. Keep your hood up and don't talk to anyone. I'll kid on that I saw you jump over the side. I'll phone the police and ambulance, I'll give a statement and show them your belongings. Then I'll watch them search for you only to announce they can't find you. It's good when its high tide and pitch black as well."

Jacob nodded and began walking away from his new 'friend' he watched as he disappeared into the darkness, then he began his plan. The Erskine Bridge was very quiet, but he saw in the distance a few cars heading towards him. He raced over to where 'Jacob jumped in' bent over the railings and then pulled himself back up, just in time for the couple of cars to come up over the small hill. He waved his arms as if he was trying to fly and the cars came to a sudden halt. He raced over to the first car. "Please call the emergency services – a guy has just jumped!"

The young female of the car pulled out her mobile phone and began dialling 999. "Hello – hi someone has just jumped off the Erskine Bridge can you send police or somebody please. Yes, we are parked, a man stopped us - he's here with us. OK thanks." She hung up on the operator and both her and the driver got out. Hazard lights went on both cars and the other driver and passenger got out of their car. They huddled up to each other, starring over the side into the murky depths of the abyss. But they all saw nothing, it was too dark anyway.

The River Clyde was a scary place, and if it swallowed someone up it would take days, sometimes months, before it decided to let the victim out.

Within seconds police arrived, followed by an ambulance crew and in the distance they all heard the coast guard's helicopter whirling in the night sky. The police shone their flashlights over the side but also saw nothing. The helicopter whirled in the dark sky and shone their high powered light down onto the water, but yet again saw nothing.

A policeman went over to the crowd and asked who was the first person to see the man jump. Needless to say he stepped forward. The police officer took him away from the crowd and began asking him questions.

"Can I take your name please?"

He looked at him. "Yeah sure, it's Zach – Zach Bushward," he lied.

He also gave a false address and then lied about what he saw. He pointed over to the railings and pointed out the various artefacts which 'the jumper' left behind.

He was thanked by the officer and then was told, along with the crowd, to go home. He nodded and left the emergency services to clean up the fake jumper. He watched firstly as they bagged Jacob's belongings and knew within the next hour they would contact his mother and break the news, and hopefully at the same time, his dear old mummy would find his suicide note and that'll be it - case closed.

Now as he smiled, he walked down into Old Kilpatrick and made his way to meet his friend. Zach Light had big plans for his new friend, big plans that involved setting him up for the various murders that he was going to commit before finally getting to his mother and father.

Darkness had descended on the small town of Clydebank but the evil light shone through it.

27
The News
22nd July 2000

Clydebank Post
ANOTHER VICTIM
CLAIMED BY THE ERSKINE BRIDGE
By James McFarlane

Last night (July 21st) another poor soul was claimed by the River Clyde.

Strathclyde police and other emergency services, including an ambulance and the coast guard, were called to the Erskine Bridge by a distressed caller, who called regarding being stopped by another member of the public who saw a young man proceed to climb the security railing and throw himself off.

Unfortunately, the young man's body was not found, although police divers are continuing their search today.

Jacob Kane, a young man from Bowling, took his life as the police believe he was emotionally stressed due to the loss of his wife, who was murdered along with a man and a young four year old boy back in February of this year.

Police are still working on the case, but haven't found their

killer yet. Police believe that Mr Kane had had enough and
wanted to be with his beloved wife again. Although at one time
was he considered a suspect in the triple murder case.

Now Mr Kane will never know who killed his wife that fateful
night in February.

Mr Kane leaves behind a baby daughter, who is now being
cared for by his mother.

A small service for friends and family will take place at
Dalnotter Cemetery a week from today (July 29th).

Zach came into his living room smiling; Kane sat on the couch
playing with his new camcorder that had been stolen from
Aldi; shoplifting was becoming too easy for Zach now. He had
stolen three camcorders and money from the cashier: sold two
camcorders, bought food and drugs for himself and gave the
other camcorder to his new friend, as a way of buttering him
up for his quest to kill his parents.

"What you smiling at?" Kane quizzed.

He walked over to Kane and sat down next to him. He
handed him the newspaper and laughed, "You're fucking
famous mate!"

Kane took the paper, read the article and his eyes went wide.

"You are now officially dead, well according to the police

that is!" he declared. "We pulled off a fake suicide, just so you can get away with murder mate. You were literally the only suspect in your wife's murder case; they were going to catch you anyway."

"I don't know what to feel." Kane stood up and started pacing the living room. "I don't know if I should feel happy or sad, or over the moon or rotten that I've left Rebecca without parents."

He stood up, putting an arm round Kane's neck. "Kane – your mum is going to look after Rebecca, if you didn't commit suicide so to speak, well the police would have charged you with the triple murder. You would be rotting in Greenock prison or Barlinnie now with no chance of parole. You would be deemed as a triple murderer. Your baby girl would have been taken off your mum and put into social services as they would have thought she shouldn't be growing up in a family where her dad killed her mum, a man and a four year old boy. You, my friend, are a genius, a crafty mother-fucking genius!" he smiled and sat back down.

Kane nodded. "Anyway you're not going to tell anyone what I done are you?"

He looked up. "No you jackass, if I told people about what you done, then I would be questioned due to the fact I planned your suicide and saw you murder your wife."

Kane smiled. "So what do you want me to do for you?" he sat back down next to him.

He smiled at him. "All in good time my friend, all in good time."

28
The Third Victim
17th August 2000

The place was buzzing with news media, reporters, police and members of the public. He stood in the crowd watching the action, he stood alone. Kane stayed in the house. (He was apparently dead after all.) Police tape surrounded the house, news media littered the streets. He was proud.

At the corner of his eye, he saw a news reporter begin to speak in front of the camera.

"Good morning, I'm John Fitzgerald reporting live from Dumbarton Road in Dalmuir where a gruesome discovery took place in the early hours of this morning."

He smiled, listening to the reporter.

"Danielle Winchester, a sixteen year old pupil of St Columbus High School, was found beaten and stabbed to death in her bedroom by her mother Denise Winchester. Mrs Winchester a widow of four years was unable to make a comment, but is being comforted by friends and family members."

He loved this.

"Police believe that the attacker climbed in through the opened window of Danielle's bedroom and murdered her while she slept. Police also believe that the killer has taken a souvenir, that being her kidney, but that is still to be confirmed."

He smirked.

"Right now as you can see behind me, police are not letting anyone through and not answering any questions until later. Forensics are on sight and hope to find clues as to why this young beautiful high school girl was attacked and murdered in cold blood in her bedroom, without anyone noticing anything suspicious."

He wanted to dance, to jump around, to shout 'it was me, me, ME!' But he wanted to wait – just a while.

"I would like to introduce Chief Inspector Alex Grimm of the Clydebank division of Strathclyde police. Chief Grimm, can you confirm anything to our viewers at the moment?"

He watched as a big burly man stood next to the reporter. He watched him with ease and watched him struggle to come to terms with what has happened. Then came the big question.

"Is this murder related to the last two murders Chief Grimm? I mean the murder of the old aged pensioner in January, followed by the young woman in February?"

He smiled as the Chief of police stuttered.

"We are not relating this murder to the two victims back at the beginning of the year," Grimm told the keen reporter.

"But is it possible that it could be the same killer for all three victims?" the reporter asked.

"Firstly," the Chief of police began, "all murders were committed differently. Secondly, what you are saying or telling your viewers is that a serial killer is running around Clydebank in this day and age!"

"But Chief Grimm," the reporter began, "what if it is a serial killer?"

The Chief of police began to walk away from the reporter. The cameraman followed Alex Grimm as he ducked under the police tape and made his way over to his officers and forensics.

He watched, smiled and turned to a middle aged man standing next him. "Crazy fucked up shit ain't it?"

The man just nodded.

He turned back to watch the reporter finish off his live report and that's when he saw him, standing there next to another officer; standing there literally directing the forensics in and out of the crime scene house.

A man he hadn't seen since 1990.

A man he swore he would hunt down and kill for what he done to him and Andrew.

The man he use to call –

Dad.

29
The Letter
17th August 2000

He sat down on his shabby couch while Kane watched the TV, he felt angry; rage built up inside. He was looking for his dad, and knew he worked here in this town he called home. But he wasn't expecting him to be a police officer. But he knew that was just a wee bonus. Hell, if he could kill a young girl, he can kill a police officer!

Surely.

He looked at Kane and pondered the question that racked his maniacal brain - should he enlist Kane in another killing spree?

Kane for what he was – a wife killer, a child killer and all round triple murderer - thought that Zach Light just murdered one person, that being the teenage girl – what was her name? He forgot, but it didn't bother him one bit. She was just another victim in his path of destruction. In his path to the killing of his father, and then his mother. His ultimate goal – to simply save Andrew from a life time of this. He knew he couldn't go out and just kill his pussy of a dad and then head home to his mum and kill her. He planned it right, well apart from the drugs that he needed and the voices in his head. He did have a plan. The only downside was Kane. He knew Kane was capable of killing, a powerhouse of pure evil, but he was far worse. To continue his plan he constructed a letter to be sent to his police officer father. To Police Officer William Light. He sat on the couch with a piece of A4 paper in front of him on the table and cut out letters from different newspapers and magazines. He had a pair of latex gloves on.

Rule number 1 – no DNA to get onto said material.

Rule number 2 – never write out letter, especially in this day and age.

And then there is Rule number 3 – the comparison to another killer.

He already declared he was the modern day Jack the Ripper, so why not continue that and let the police force know that they are dealing with one fucked up individual.

He began to pick up various letters from the alphabet and constructed the letter. Once he had the letter in place, he glued it down.

"Kane what do you think?" he asked his sidekick.

Kane turned and read over the makeshift letter and smiled. "I like it mate, but seriously – your not going to eat part of the kidney are you?"

He screwed up his face. "Don't be fucking disgusting, I'm not a cannibal!" He placed the letter back on the table, smoothed it out and read it out:

Judgement Day

Mr Light

Sir,

I send you half the kidney I took from one girl preserved it for you, the other piece I fried and ate, it was very nice. I may send you the bloody knife that took it out, if you only wait a while longer. Please note, when the devil comes a calling, he will break your earthly ties. The land will break and the seas will rise. The wind will rage as it burns up the sky. All your beliefs will be broken and fall. Judgement day is coming William, cause on your final day...

I'll end it all.

Signed,

Catch me When you Can William Light.

He fell back laughing and smiling. He knew this was the start of the game, so to speak. Kane didn't know he had already killed two people prior to the young sixteen year old girl, but he was relishing in the fact that he could be bigger news than the notorious Whitechapel Murderer.

"So, you're just going to send the letter with the kidney in a box and see what happens next?" Kane asked.

He nodded. "Kane, you have to understand something, this is just a game."

"Yeah, I can see you're having fun Zach, but seriously mate – do you really want caught?" Kane questioned.

He rose up and starred down at Kane. "I'm not going to get fucking caught, if I play the game correctly!" He paced in front of Kane. "You got away with murder and lied through your teeth to the cops, and I'm just doing the exact same but on a bigger scale."

Kane rose up and stared him in the eyes. "Zach, yeah I lied and got away with murder, but only because I'm officially dead. Yeah, so I was going to throw myself off the Erskine Bridge, but that's only because the police were getting to close. You talked me down, invited me to live but act dead. I did just that! You said you wouldn't tell what you saw in the Kilpatrick hills that night back in February; you said you wouldn't speak of it if I would help you. At first when I found out what you wanted to do, I was shocked but I understood cause of what I did. But what you did to that girl was far worse

124

than what I did. Yeah, so I lied to the cops, I killed my wife, her lover and his son, but I did that out of rage, out of dishonour; you, my friend, killed that girl for pure pleasure!"

He smiled at him. "Kane, Kane, Kane, it's all a fucking game, don't you get it?"

Kane walked to the living room window, looking out and up to Clydebank train station. He turned to his friend, "I'm out!" he declared. "I don't want anything more to do with this – this thing you call a game!"

He looked at him. "Is that right? He walked over to him and looked him dead in the eyes. "You're out?"

Kane nodded. "Yeah no more for me!"

He just laughed, "Kane where the fuck are you going to go man? You're fucking dead! You can't just turn up out of the blue and say you were washed up onshore and have forgotten everything!"

Kane smiled. "That's my plan, and a risk I'll have to take. Don't worry I won't say a word, I won't blabber to the cops about your sick little game, or the fact that you pleasured yourself while watching the tape recording back. Oh and by the way, you can keep the camcorder."

He just nodded to what Kane was saying. "OK mate," he started sarcastically. "OK, that's fine with me, so you better go now. Go down to the Clyde and throw yourself in, get all wet, lose your memory and then turn up alive as such. You better leave now because frankly, you are no use to me now!"

Kane although shocked, nodded with what he was telling him. Grabbing his jacket, Kane walked towards the front door. "Listen Zach, watch what you're doing okay?"

He just stared at him, raised his hand and signalled for him to leave.

Kane opened the front door and walked out of his saviour's house. He hoped he would never see him again.

The door closed behind Kane and he stood still looking out the window. "The time has come for the game to get underway. Kane may have left, but I can survive on my own. I can do this." He turned towards the coffee table and grabbed hold of the cardboard box, which he was putting the half of kidney in - the other half wasn't eaten by him, it was simply throwing out with the rubbish. He placed the girl's kidney in the box, wrapped up nice in a napkin. Then he folded up the letter carefully and placed it in the box. He sealed it up and addressed it to:

Officer William Light

Strathclyde police

Clydebank police station

Clydebank

His next plan was to post it as far out from Clydebank as he could, he already knew where he was going to post it – in Glasgow City Centre.

He got up pulled on his black hooded top and left his house.

Game on.

30
Mother's Day
2nd April 2000

Mothering Sunday, a day when you thank your mother for being there, caring for you and loving you. A day where you give gifts and cards to your mother. Andrew however didn't do that, instead he was subjected to vicious abuse and neglect from his mother.

Andrew wanted to love her like a son should. But it wasn't to be.

No gifts, no cards, no love.

People across Glasgow were giving their mothers the presents they bought or made. Andrew was giving his body to the sick vile woman that was his mother.

Andrew couldn't eat, he couldn't sleep, his plan and main aim and wish was to see his mother dead, he wanted her to sleep forever, he hummed a wee verse to himself, something he came up with, 'Not another peep, you will be six feet deep, just go to sleep.' He smiled. He was just being hurt too much and knew if it continued it just wouldn't work.

For Andrew being hurt more, just wouldn't be sufficient

enough cause. He saw his mother as an enemy and as long as she was breathing there was only one thing that they could agree on and that was simply – one of them had to die.

There wasn't any reason to speak to her, because all she saw in front of her was simply a piece of meat, a sex object and Andrew wanted to stop that once and for all. So the hatred would continue until the flesh of his mother was dead. He knew he had to unleash the demon in him that no one, let alone, his mother had ever seen before. He didn't need any help; he was going to do this all by himself. He wanted rid of her, all of her, and killing her was the only option.

Andrew wanted his mother to rot! To decay in the dirt, six feet deep, that would be her depth. There would be no more pain, no more abuse once his abusive mother was gone.

Away to sleep.

This was Andrew's day. He had planned it carefully, drawn pictures of the day and had nightmares of this day.

The day in which he murders his mother.

He envisioned the *Psycho 2* scene in which Norman Bates' mother sat at the kitchen table beginning to drink her cup of tea, when Norman lifts the garden shovel and bashes her brains in.

He had the shovel just lying next to the fridge, in easy reach.

Next was getting his mother down out of her bedroom and he knew how.

Vodka – a life of near enough every alcoholic.

He climbed the stairs and walked towards his mum's bedroom; he reached for the door handle and gently opened the door. He entered and saw his mum lying in her bed - the bed where she done nasty things to him. But that was all in the past, today was the day that it all ended, the hole was dug in the back garden next to his garden swing (which was rotting away, due to him growing up now). Mud piled high and the hole lying deep.

He walked over to the bed and whispered, "Mum." She turned over and opened her eyes. "Mum – I've got a surprise for you!"

She sat up, showing that all she wore was a small silk chemise; which didn't really cover her up. "Emmm, and what is that Andrew?"

"You have to come down and get it, it's in the kitchen!" Andrew declared.

"Emmm, just give me it here son," she began, "it's not that I don't want it in the kitchen, I just prefer it in this big comfy bed, which I'm really lonely in." She patted the covers next to her signalling Andrew to come lie down with her.

But Andrew was having none of it, Zach had left back in December 1999, his dad had left in early 1990. They both were probably living much better lives, and he was being abused by his mother: the person that gave birth to him, the person he loved and adored and said he would never leave, until she started doing the sad and pathetic things she done to him.

This was simply payback.

Things ran through Andrews mind constantly. Things like: once he kills her, does he just open the front door and walk out to freedom? Does he just wander the streets until some generous good Samaritan picks him up and gives him a good home? Or does he go straight to the police and confess why he killed her?

All would be answered once he done the deed.

"Come on Mum," Andrew began, "please come down, you'll enjoy it, I guarantee it."

She flung the covers off of her and got up out of bed. "You better give the best you can son." Andrew took her by the hand and guided her down the hallway and the stairs towards the kitchen, "I even have a bottle of vodka for you!"

She smiled. "Now we are talking son, a good time and then a drink afterwards. I'm happy with that."

They both entered the kitchen, Andrew guided her to the kitchen table and sat her down. "I'll get you a glass for that vodka Mum."

"Fuck that!" she stated. "I'll drink from the bottle. Now what's my surprise?"

Andrew walked behind her, letting his hands wander over her naked shoulders. He walked over to the kitchen. "All in good time Mum, all in good time. Now close your eyes."

She did as she was told and then she felt the pain, almost as though her brain was bouncing about inside her skull. Andrew reined blow, after blow, after blow of the shovel down upon his abusive mother, his captor. She fell to the floor, her body shaking violently as he continued battering her around the head. Blood started to pool under her, covering her silk chemise as it soaked up the red liquid.

Andrew reigned another three, maybe four blows down on his now dying mother. "Arghhhhhhhhh! Go to sleep bitch, die motherfucker die!"

His mother stopped moving and he stopped swinging the shovel like a baseball bat. He placed the shovel back against the wall at the fridge; it was time to take out the trash once and for all.

He grabbed hold of her legs and began pulling her across the kitchen floor, leaving a nice trail of blood in his wake. He dragged her out into the back garden and over to the deep muddy hole. He rolled her into it and she fell deep into the muddy hole with a thud. He went back into the kitchen and grabbed hold of the shovel and the vodka. He went back out to the hole and began shovelling the dirt onto his dead mother. "Go to sleep bitch, take a nap." He shovelled more and more of the dirt on top of his mother and then noticed her fingers twitching.

"What the-?" he said out loud stunned. Andrew jumped down into the hole and stood above the twitching carcass. He raised the shovel and brought it forcefully down on his dying prey and with one quick slice he pushed the shovel through his mother's neck, snapping her head from the rest of the body like it was a lollipop stick. Blood sprayed all around him, making the dirt wetter. He noticed that the first spray of blood that went over her silk chemise had turned a nice shade of orange, but now was covered with fresh blood.

Andrew climbed out of the hole, looked down at his dead mother and began covering her with the remaining dirt. He packed it down and sat down on the grass surrounding the grave. He opened the bottle of vodka, took a swig from it and poured the rest into the new grave. "Happy Mother's Day

Mum!"

31
There's a Serial Killer on the Loose
19th August 2000

THE DAILY RECORD
ANOTHER MURDER IN CLYDEBANK
By
Robin Mason

The town of Clydebank, West Dunbartonshire was rocked by the latest murder to happen in their small town.

Earlier this week, a young girl of sixteen years of age was found stabbed and battered to death in her own bed.

Danielle Winchester, a St Columbus High school pupil, with her whole life in front of her, was struck down by an unseen attacker. Police are piecing together what evidence they have uncovered at the scene.

Earlier this year, another TWO murders were committed in and around Clydebank, causing this to be the THIRD murder in as little as SIX months.

Police have stated that they don't believe the murders to be related, but they haven't ruled anything out.

More will follow on this case once it is revealed.

He sat down on the old bench at the Forth and Clyde canal, just down a bit from the West Dunbartonshire Council building. It was a warm day, around 21C, a nice warm Saturday morning.

He glanced through the rest of the paper until he got to the sport at the back pages. His beloved Glasgow Rangers were playing away at Fife against Dunfermline and he was going to catch the game on the TV in John Browns pub.

He smiled as he turned back to the front page and saw the lovely beautiful photo of his victim Danielle staring out at him from the newspaper.

"You loved it, didn't you?" he whispered to the photo. "You loved me standing over you and beating you to a pulp. You wanted it and asked for it, but you also wanted me to fuck you hard. But I didn't do that to you, didn't want to leave my DNA on you!"

An old man walked past him, as his Labrador jumped into the cesspit of the canal.

The old man looked at him but then turned his eyes back to his dog. "Snowy, come on boy!"

He looked up at the old man. "You got a staring problem old man?"

The old man didn't say a word; he began walking slightly

faster than normal. Zach got up off the bench and began walking behind him.

The old man glanced back at his stalker. "Listen son, go bug someone else." The old man's dog came jumping out of the water and ran next to his master.

He didn't stop; he just continued walking towards the old man. The old man stopped and spun round to come face to face with his attacker.

He just stood still as the old man glared at him. "What do you want?"

He cocked his head from one side to the other side.

The old man's dog growled at him.

"Answer me you fucking wee toe-rag!" was all the old man got to say.

He lunged at the old timer and started repeatedly stabbing him with something. Blood splashed him and splashed the gravel path below them as the old man tried to suck in as much air as possible. He backed away from the old timer and showed him what he was being stabbed with - a Stanley blade.

The old man reached both hands to his stomach, clutching at the gapping wounds left by the simple cutting tool. He fell to his knees next to his beloved companion and stared up at his attacker. "Why?" he gasped.

"To see what you insides looked like!" was his response.

The old timer slumped to all fours, and blood dripped happily from his stomach wounds. The dog growled at him and bared its teeth. Then it leapt at him knocking the blade out of his hand and into the murky water of the canal. He fell onto the hard gravel below, feeling the sharp pain as the gravel stones stuck into his body. The dog was trying to tear shreds off him, but to no avail.

He held his sleeve up and the dog held on to it with his teeth: growling, scratching and trying to tear flesh from him.

He wrestled with the dog and raised his fist and punched the dog in the face. The dog whimpered and got off of him. He scrambled to his feet, and volleyed the dog in ribs; the dog yet again let out a cry, unable to growl or bite now as he lifted his leg and brought it forcefully down on his cowering prey. Foot after foot came crashing down on the poor defenceless animal, and then it fell to the ground in one giant lump of hair.

He cocked his head to the right and bent down over the animal, put both of his hands around the dog's neck and twisted it till he heard the bones snap. "Hush now little doggy." He stood up and kicked the dog into the water, watching it sink into the dark abyss of the canal. He then turned his attention to the old man, who was dying a slow painful death. He walked over to his victim and looked down at him. "Not so big now are you old man?" He kicked him in order for him to roll onto his back.

"Ple...please don't kill me!" the old man gasped. "I won't tell!"

"Damn right you won't tell!" he exclaimed before raising his boot and bringing it forcefully down on the man's head until it caved in. He then did the exact same to the man as he had done to the dog - rolled him into the stinking water that made up the canal. He watched as his newest victim sunk into the darkness. He then walked back to the bench, picked up his paper and walked away back home.

Four bodies plus a dog now lay in his wake and along with the voices in his head guiding him to his father, more were sure to follow.

He was now a certified serial killer.

He smiled. "Just call me Jack!"

32
Andrew Has Seen the Light
23rd April 2000

Andrew sat in the café. He felt out of place - it was the first time in a long time since he had actually been out the house!

Drinking a coffee and watching the small portable TV that perched on a shelf above the counter, Andrew watched the STV lunchtime news. All they seemed to be talking about was the triple murders of people found in a house down near Bowling in West Dunbartonshire, that and the murders of a old woman and a young woman back at the beginning of the year.

Andrew sipped at his coffee, blowing the steam off the cup. He had thought of going to the police and telling them that his mum had sexual, physically and mentally abused him since his older brother left the house, and that his dad was nowhere to be seen. But that was a big no-no. He didn't want people knowing what he had been through. Most of all, he didn't want people knowing that he had bashed his mum's brains in, decapitated her and buried her in the back garden.

Thoughts went through his mind: he was a monster, a diabolical monster.

Andrew didn't want to be the centre of attention; he didn't want some idiotic shrink telling him that he was bad and needed to be locked up in Gartnaval or Carstairs.

He watched the people float about him with not a care in the world, not knowing that they all sat or stood near a killer. Yeah so what if he was a killer? A one off killer at that, but he wasn't like the person running about killing innocent people. He simply killed his bitch of a mother - and not before long!

Andrew nearly finished his coffee. When he saw the young café worker turn the TV over to MTV and on the screen was a dark video. He watched it intrigued with the beat that went with the video. Then the song kicked in and he saw his life flash before his eyes. The chorus bared a slight resemblance to him.

The first few lines stuck in his head and he began to sing along to it.

Andrew missed the name of the song and band, so stood up and walked to the counter. "Excuse me?" he said to the young girl behind the counter, while she whistled away to the song. "Who sings this?"

The girl looked up and smiled. "It's a band called ATB."

"What's the name of the song?" he asked.

"Killer." She told him.

He smiled, turned and left, he had indeed related himself to the song. Now he was going to look for his big brother, he wanted to be with his brother and live with him. But the tricky part was trying to find him first of all.

Andrew sang the catchy chorus again as he walked out the café to himself He smiled.

33
You've Got Mail
20th August 2000

People crowded round his desk wanting to know what the parcel was. William Light read the name on the box:

To William Light

Clydebank Police Office

Montrose Street

Clydebank

West Dunbartonshire

The postmark read:

Glasgow

And was dated:

18th August 2000

It was sealed by tape and sealed really tight. William was handed some latex gloves and proceeded to put them on, he then took a knife and began cutting open the box.

The crowd of cops gathered in silence round the desk as William pulled open the lids of the box, inside contained a letter on top of what looked like a shoebox of some kind. William pulled the letter out and held it in both hands – puzzled he placed the box to one side and placed the letter flat on the desk. He held down one side and opened up the letter and stared at it, he read it over and over again. Then he looked up, his face drained of all colour. "What the fuck?"

He closed the letter over and moved the box into position in front of him, he reached in and removed the lid on the other box and there lying staring up at him was half a kidney.

He pushed the box away as the putrid smell engulfed him and his fellow officers. He stood up feeling sick, turned to his waste paper bin and puked up his breakfast. Wiping his mouth, he stood up. "Get me forensics; I want them to check the box for DNA, fingerprints, anything!" A rookie officer looking ever so pale as well, nodded and went and fetched a team member from the forensics department. William looked at each officer. "Well back to your desks, for Christ sake!"

The other officers all turned and walked away from William as he himself made a beeline to his Chief's office.

Chapping on the door and awaiting response, he entered as soon as he was allowed. "Alex – it is a serial killer!" he declared.

Alex looked up and nodded, "I know."

William closed the door and sat down on the black leather chair facing his boss. "We got to do something fast. And anyway how do you know?"

Alex got up out of his chair and paced around the room. "After that girl was found, I knew we had a serial killer in our town William." He stopped pacing and stared out of the window down onto the Kilbowie Retail Park which was once home to his beloved Clydebank Football Club. It was bulldozed in the late 90s due to liquidation. Alex turned and faced William. "Two killings literally weeks apart, then a break and then the girl. The killings are getting more vicious as this killer escalades."

William looked at him. "So what do we do?"

Alex walked back to the desk and sat back down; he placed his elbows on the desk and balanced his head in his palms. "We have to call in a serial killer profiler, one from Strathclyde University. All I know is this killer is killing girls and woman so far. That's three bodies that I didn't want to join the dots together with, but I knew, I knew that it was a serial killer."

William gulped some saliva down his dry throat. "The letter Alex, the fucking letter and a half of a kidney, half of the fucking little girl's kidney!"

This time the colour drained from Alex'S face. "What letter?"

William stood up. "Come and I'll show you."

Alex stood up and followed his best mate out into the corridor and followed him towards Williams's desk. Alex proceeded, pulled on a pair of latex gloves and looked over the letter and then looked into the box and saw the kidney. "Sick motherfucker!" Alex declared. "He's fucking taunting us now, telling us yes we have a serial killer. Fucking bastard!"

William put a hand on his friend's shoulder. "We will get him, we will get him sooner rather than later!"

Alex nodded. "Once we get it analyzed by our forensic squad, we will call in a profiler and then release a statement to the media. Maybe someone somewhere will have some information."

William nodded. "Hopefully."

34
I Was Lost, Now I'm Found
18th August 2000

Jacob Kane stood at the bottom of the driveway, staring up at his mother's house. Shadows danced in front of the living room window, he saw the outline of his beautiful daughter getting swung about. He heard the soft giggling coming from her tiny mouth.

Jacob thought that this would be the most awkward moment of his whole life. Firstly his wife dead, and being accused of the murder; not proven however. Then he was going to commit suicide only to be saved by (at the time) his saviour, and now he stands at the bottom of his mother's driveway, about to embark on the scariest part ever – telling his mum that he survived jumping off the Erskine Bridge.

Would she believe it?

It was time to find out.

Jacob checked himself over once again.

Unshaven – check.

Ripped and wet clothes – check.

Dishevelled hair – check.

He walked up the driveway, took a deep breath, raised his fist and chapped the front door. He heard a muffled, "Now Rebecca you watch the *Tweenies* while Nanna answers the door." A little bit of noise followed and light footsteps approached him from the other side of the door. He breathed deeply again and heard his mother with a shocked cry, "Oh my God!" She opened the front door and looked into the eyes of her only son. "Jacob! Oh my God! It's you! It's really you! Come in. Come in." She grabbed his hand and pulled him in, closing the door behind him. She embraced him with a strong heart-warming cuddle. "Look at you. Look at the state of you. Where were you? I – we thought you were dead!"

"Mum-" Jacob began.

"Hot shower," she cut in, "that's what you need. A hot shower, clean clothes and some of your mum's hot chocolate. After that you can see your daughter. Sound good?"

"Mum-" Jacob said again.

"You can fill me in later," she cut in again. "Come on, let me run you that shower." She held his hand tightly and guided him past the living room, where Rebecca sat watching her programmes, and up to the bathroom. She went in and turned on the shower.

"There you go son," she began, "you get in there and have a

relaxing shower, towels are in the cabinet as normal and I'll get you fresh clothes. I'll meet you down stairs with a relaxing mint flavoured hot chocolate." She patted his hand and ushered him into the bathroom, she began to close the door.

"Mum-" Jacob began again.

"Hush now son, shower then we will talk." She closed the door and began her walk down the stairs.

Jacob locked the bathroom door, placed his two hands onto the back of the door and rested his head against them. He didn't know how he was going to tell his dear old mum how he survived the 100 foot fall from the bridge - where it has been proven that your body can shut down before you hit the ground or water. Jacob turned to the shower, steam rising into the air swirling around him like dancing fog. He removed all his old dirty clothes and climbed into the shower, the hot water cascading down his body.

Since leaving Zach's house he had pondered on how he would cope doing this. Questions ran through his mind.

Will the police come knocking again?

Will they question him once more and come to the conclusion that he faked his death because they were getting too close to him?

But if they did that, wouldn't they want to find and speak to the man that said he 'saw' him jump?

Which means they will dig deeper and find out about Zach and then put two and two together and put him with Zach at the teenage girl's bedroom where Zach murdered her?

Jacob promised Zach he wouldn't tell the police anything. He knew he had to say that he lost his memory, doesn't remember one thing. Has to play on that, until piece by piece his memory comes back.

He lathered himself with Dove shower cream (his mum's favourite), getting all the dirt and grime off his naked body. He washed his hair and started shaving his beard that had started to grow.

About ten minutes later, he stopped the shower and got out, grabbing the towel, he dried off and wrapped the towel round him. He unlocked the door and outside the bathroom door was a set of clothes. He picked them up, closed the door again and began to get dressed. He breathed hard; it was now time to lie to his mum one more time.

35
Andrew Finds His Dad
4th May 2000

It was a cold Thursday morning. The rain bounced off the ground. Andrew walked along the pavement that ran alongside Maryhill Road. He passed by the BP garage and saw the sign reading:

NEXT LEFT DRUMCHAPEL

He planned on finding his dad and today was the day. He remembered his dad telling him and Zach stories when they were young of his childhood in Drumchapel: The places he played, the school he went to, the laughs he had with his friends. Andrew had thought that Drumchapel was the place that his dad would return to after walking out on him, his brother and his mother.

Andrew had no money left. The money he paid for the coffee in that small café was now gone. So he walked for a bit, then when night fell, he found a place to sleep. There was no way he could go to a homeless shelter or the police, because one thing was certain – they would ask where his parents were. The scenario played through his mind umpteen times:

Police officer - "Where's your parents, son?

Him - "Well dad left back in 1990 and well my mum – she's dead and buried in my back garden with her head chopped off!"

There was no way he was going to the authorities, so he walked and walked. He clutched a piece of paper and looked at it constantly; it read: 16 Southdeen Avenue.

That was his dad's address he gathered, because one day, mail came to the house and he heard his mother tell the postman, "He doesn't stay here anymore – his new address is 16 Southdeen Avenue in Drumchapel." Andrew took a note of it and knew one day he would get out to find his father. Not for revenge, but to feel love from his dad. He knew it wasn't his dad's fault for walking out on his sons; he just couldn't cope with her – the witch that caused all the problems.

He clutched the paper with all his might and turned onto Bearsden Road leading to Drumchapel. It took a further thirty minutes (at least) before he saw the sign - WELCOME TO DRUMCHAPEL. He turned onto Kinfauns Drive and stopped for a breather. A teenage girl passed by him.

"Excuse me," Andrew asked.

"Yeah what's up?" the cute girl answered.

"Can you tell me where Southdeen Avenue is?"

The girl turned and pointed across a green field where a pair of goal posts stood. Past the goals stood a street. "That's it there."

Andrew nodded, "Thanks."

He continued on his way, this time walking across the grass which wasn't exactly dry. Mud puddles lined the edging; he dodged them but still got covered in mud. He wasn't exactly a pretty sight!

Andrew now stood in front of a set of stairs leading up to a controlled entry door. He breathed hard and began walking up the steps of 16 Southdeen Avenue, home of his dad, his dad he hasn't seen in over ten years. He scrolled his fingers over the list of names in bold that resided in the four storey, terraced house:

4/1: S. King	4/2: S. Cunningham
3/1: C. Barker	3/2: J. Carpenter
2/1: D. Bradley	2/2: C. Robertson
1/1: D. Koontz	1/2: R. Stine
0/1: W. Light	0/2: W. Craven

His finger rested on 0/1: W. Light, which was him, it had to be.

Andrew had found his father.

It had taken him over ten years: years of neglect from his mother, years of abuse. Not able to get away, but finally he had. Finally he was rid of the evil that stayed in that house in Summerston. He pushed the buzzer and waited, someone said something through the speaker but it was muffled so the door automatically opened. Andrew walked up the small close entrance, turned to his left and knocked on the door marked *W. Light*.

He waited no longer than one minute, when the door opened. A little girl stood in front of him: a frilly dress and her hair in pigtails. She held a brown teddy bear.

"Hello little girl is my…um…can I speak to William Light please?"

The little girl looked up at him. "My daddy is at work, he's a policeman!"

Andrew gulped some dry air down his throat. "Your…your daddy?"

"Yes my daddy – Police Officer William Light." She stood to attention, hand up to her forehead as if she was saluting him.

"Is your…um…mum home?" he forced out.

"MUMMMMMMMMMMMMMMM," she screamed,

154

almost deafening him.

He heard noise come from behind the little girl as a beautiful woman in her late twenties came into view. She was wearing a tight t-shirt, that showed off her figure, over black leggings, her blonde hair cascaded down onto her shoulders. "Can I help you son?"

Son! he thought. *I ain't your son!*

"I'm looking for William Light," he declared again.

"And who are you?" the woman asked, pushing her daughter behind her.

"I'm...uh...I'm...his...his...I'm   just   a   friend!" He stammered through. "Can you tell him that Andrew called to see him? If he wants to see me I'll be up next to the Spar shop on Bearsden Road."

The woman looked puzzled but nodded her head. "OK Andrew, I'll pass the message on. He should be home soon." She smiled and closed the door.

Andrew bowed his head and a single tear ran down his cheek.

He turned and walked back out of the close, down the stairs and back up over the muddy grass. He kept thinking to himself, surely it was a different William Light? *It had to be! Surely to God his dad didn't walk out and then found a new woman and had a baby with her?*

He knew he had to wait until this woman passed on the information before he would have the chance to finally meet this man he hoped but didn't hope was his dad.

But waiting was a nightmare.

36
The Profiler
23rd August 2000

"There are various different serial killers out there," Ellen Scott told the room of police officers. Ellen was a lecturer from Strathclyde University who lectured on serial killer profiling. She was drafted in to help Clydebank police officers with their case against the recent spat of killings. "After carefully looking over the crime scenes and victims, you will see that each victim is being mutilated worse than the last one. However there does stand common traits between each and every different serial killer. Usually you will find that serial killer tendencies begin in early childhood, you can look for this with common problems ranging from bed wetting, injuring or even killing small animals and setting fire. Children that tend to be abused can turn their animal instinct towards murdering human beings."

Police officers crammed into the room, sat on chairs taking notes down from what the lecturer was telling them. William Light sat in the front row with the Chief of police sitting next to him. "Excuse me Ellen?" William began. "We don't know much about this killer, can you elaborate a bit more?"

Ellen stood up and moved to a white board at the front of the room, she began writing but still speaking at the same time. "Potential serial killers have a desire to be alone when older, they have the inability to do well at school, in some cases not even attending school. Holding a job down is sometimes a problem as well and yet again in some instances they don't even have a job."

"But what if we don't know any of this?" a middle aged officer spoke up from the back of the room. "What I mean is we have no evidence, no DNA, we simply don't have anything, no fingerprints. Nothing – so how the hell do we find this son of a bitch and stop them?"

Ellen turned and looked out at the sea of bodies in front of her. "Serial killers tend to kill in a series. Usually one kill comes one month and then they wait awhile before committing another murder, however some serial murderers tend to kill, then kill again before taking a break. This is known as a spree killer. A killer that wants to make a point, is full of rage and will not stop until they are caught or die. That's what is happening here in Clydebank. This killer is not going to strike in the same place again, they will move about almost like a travelling killer. But what you are dealing with is what we call a Visionary Serial Killer – a serial killer who hears voices that tell them to kill other humans, they are usually psychotic or schizophrenic. Let's look at the victims. Victim number one had her eye gouged out, almost like the killer is telling you to 'see no evil', victim number two was stabbed through the neck almost like they were saying 'speak no evil', but the third victim throws me: this young girl was battered to death and stabbed numerous times then her kidney removed, apparently half was eaten and the other half mailed to officer William Light here."

"So what does this mean Ellen?" William asked.

Ellen looked at him. "It means this killer is changing their plans of attack, from organised to disorganised. This means they are attacking when they want and who they want. Looking at various facts available in any giving text book on serial killers, we are mostly looking for a man between the ages of eighteen to thirty five of a white ethic background, who either stays local or knows the town well. Maybe travels to and from this area on any giving day throughout the week."

Words could not be said stronger than those last few sentences. Words that will ring true with William Light sooner than he thinks.

37
Bonnie and Clyde 2000
18th August 2000

"It's just us baby girl," Jacob whispered as he carried his daughter to the car, "Nobody is going to keep us apart." Jacob opened up the back door of the car and placed his daughter in the car seat. It was time to see how far his mother could throat. Kane was simply getting rid of the baggage that he didn't need anymore.

Jacob climbed into the driver's seat and closed the door; he started up the engine and pulled out of his mother's driveway. It wasn't that long ago when he turned up, 'back from the dead', so to speak at his mother's door and was welcomed in, no questions asked. He had a shower while his mum kept his daughter busy. He got ready and headed down the stairs to the living room. He sat down on the leather two-seater across from his mother who perched on her recliner, Rebecca played on the sheepskin rug at the fireplace.

"Mum I have to tell you something…I-" Jacob began.

"Do you want a cup of tea son?" his mum cut in. She stood up, smiling down at her grand-daughter. She began walking towards the kitchen.

"Mum, I have to say something!" Jacob began again, standing up and moving to the kitchen with his mum.

His mum busied herself making up two cups of tea. "Emmm?"

"Mum, I-" Jacob began again.

"How do you take your tea again son?" she cut in.

Jacob began to get angry, blood pumped through him and his blood pressure rose dramatically.

"Mum, I-" Jacob began one more time.

"I know exactly what you did Jacob," his mum said facing away from him, making the cups up. Jacob stood there, mouth opened. "You killed her didn't you?"

Jacob gulped, his mouth dry, no saliva passed over his tongue. It felt as though he was swallowing razor blades.

"Didn't you?" his mum said. She turned round to face him. "And then you faked your own death so the police wouldn't arrest you! How could you do that son? How could you do that to me? To your daughter?"

Three questions he just could not answer. He gulped again. "Mum, she was having an affair!"

She looked him right in the eyes, "And that gives you the right to kill her? Rebecca's mother! Your wife! Not only that, but you killed her lover and what seems to be his son. What the hell was going through your mind?"

But hell was exactly what was going through Jacob's mind. He was in hell from the moment he walked into his house and caught them having sex, not making love like a husband and wife do, but hard at it; like two animals in the jungle, with not a care in the world.

"Mum, I-" he was cut short once more. This was making his blood boil.

"I'm phoning the police," his mum declared. "You have to hand yourself in!" she made her way towards the phone which hung on the wall above the chest freezer.

He looked on and sighed. He couldn't let his mum do this, he couldn't let his mum phone the police and rat out her son. He walked over to the kitchen sink and bowed his head as he picked up the serrated kitchen knife. His mum faced the wall, dialling the local police station as he walked up behind her.

"Mum put the phone down!" he declared but she ignored him. "Mum please put the phone down!" he asked again, yet again she ignored him. He sighed as he pulled the serrated blade across her throat from right to left; she spun round dropping the receiver. She gurgled the blood in her throat, looking at her son, looking at her killer. She held a hand to her throat and the other was held out, pleading to her son to help her.

"I'm sorry Mum," Jacob began, "I can't go to jail or prison, yes so I attempted suicide but someone saved me and I came back for Rebecca, for my baby. I may not go to heaven but I'm sure as hell not going to jail!" His mother slumped against the wall, the phone receiver dangling behind her with a dialling tone coming from it. He dropped the knife and stared at his mother's lifeless corpse.

His fourth kill.

Back in the car, driving along the road, he looked in his rear-view mirror. He smiled at his daughter and reassured her that when she was older, he might explain what he had done.

Rebecca fell asleep and Jacob continued to watch the road, and watch his daughter in the mirror as he drove along towards Loch Lomond. His plan was simple: his mother was going to be thrown into the Loch where she would eventually be washed out with the tide into the North Sea, sooner or later. Jacob didn't like doing this, he didn't want to kill his mother, but he had no choice. She was going to hand him in to the police, where he would be tried and sentenced to life in prison, and for once he wasn't going to be the fall guy.

He parked the car just north of the entrance to the Balloch

Hotel. Got out and opened the trunk, Kane pulled out his dead mother and carried her over to the pier. He laid her down and went back to get his daughter. He got her out of the car and carried her over to where he placed his dead mother. She woke up as he put her down on the ground. She watched as he rolled her grandmother off the pier and they both watched as the dead body sunk to the bottom of the Loch

Jacob walked back to the trunk of the car to retrieve the serrated knife and the bloody clothes he was wearing when he slit his mum's throat. He walked back towards Rebecca and watched as his dear old mother sank to the bottom of the Loch. He threw in the knife, after giving it a clean so no fingerprints were left on it, and threw that along with the clothes into the dark abyss that now hid another two items.

Jacob picked his daughter up and carried her back to the car; he placed her into the car seat and fastened the seatbelt. He got in himself and started the engine, he smiled into the mirror at his young offspring. Jacob drove the car away; he knew he couldn't live around Clydebank, Bowling or Old Kilpatrick anymore, hell he even knew he couldn't live anywhere in Glasgow. (He was officially dead anyway!) Plus he didn't want to be anywhere near this place when things began to heat up with his so called saviour Zach Light. So his plan was simple: grab clothes for his daughter and things for himself and head away from Glasgow, away from Scotland and start a new life. Just him and his daughter.

38
A Surprise for William
4th May 2000

"Honey I'm home," William called as he entered the front door of his terraced house. A nice little house that he shared with his fiancée and his little girl.

Things were finally getting better for William: he left his past where it stayed forever, his boys, his wife – all gone. It took him a long time to forget about his boys, but they had had the chance to go with him and be happy here with him and his new family.

He was now happy to be back in his home town of Drumchapel. He always wanted to work with the police force and applied to Drumchapel police station, but was sent to a position in Clydebank police station. It was only twenty minutes away and he loved it. He was now firmly a pillar of the community.

William walked into the living room and sat down on the black three seater sofa across from his fiancée who sat on the single black chair next to the boiler cupboard. *The Tweenies* played on the TV as his young daughter sat in front of the fire with her Barbie dolls in front of her.

"How was your day honey?" William asked his new woman.

She looked up from her TV magazine. "A weird sort of a day, we had a visitor at the door, a young boy covered in mud, he was actually really smelly, he claims he is friends with you!"

William looked puzzled. "Who was it?"

His fiancée just shook her head. "Don't know, he didn't give me his name."

William stood up and looked out the window across the greenery on the other side of the road. "Come on Nancy, surely he gave you a name!"

Nancy, his fiancée, stood up and moved towards him, putting her arms around his waist. "Sorry babe I didn't ask, but he did say he would meet you up at the Spar shop on Bearsden Road – if that's any help."

William turned round. "When was he here?"

Nancy looked up at the wall clock. "A few hours ago, he says he would wait."

William gave his fiancée a kiss on the lips. "I'll go up and see who it is." He grabbed his coat from the sofa, bent down and gave his daughter a kiss on the head. "I won't be long." He made his way to the front door, hearing Nancy shout,

"Don't be, dinner will be ready in about an hour." He nodded and closed the front door behind him.

Outside, William didn't bother taking his car up to the shop, it was only a ten minute walk. He didn't bother going over the soggy grass, instead he walked round the road and up Kinfauns Drive. He eventually got to Spar after walking up the make shift path through the grass field on the other-side of the road. William looked around the outskirts of the shop, he peered around the corner of the shop but still saw nothing. He shrugged and was beginning to walk away when he heard a young boy's voice call out, "So you changed huh? You've got a phone; you could have picked it up and called me!"

William spun round. A young boy in dirty clothes stared up at him from the steps that led to the hair dressers above the Spar shop. Gobsmacked, William moved closer. "Andrew?"

Andrew stood up. "Oh you remember my name do you? It's been a long time hasn't it Dad?" William gulped the saliva down into his throat; gobsmacked wasn't just the word that described what was happening right now. "Tell me Dad, how come we never talked since you left? And you didn't even call us after you had gone? And lastly, I was so looking forward to seeing you Dad. But then when I turned up at your front door and saw you had a new family that love just disappeared. All I wanted was a hug, a hug to say 'I'm still here for you Andrew'. After all these years that you've been gone, this bullshit can't be true Dad. We are family and ain't a damn thing changed except you!"

William stood in silence; he didn't know what to say, or how to respond to the hateful words sprouting from his second oldest child.

Andrew stepped towards him. "I was young and we were close – like two peas in a pod. Then Mum fell ill and you just walk out on me, on me and Zach! Why Dad? Why?"

This time William had an answer. "I asked you both to come with me and you both refused!"

Andrew shook his head. "No Dad, we didn't refuse as I remember, you shouted and we didn't answer, then you left! As much as your pride tries to hide it, you are a cold selfish bastard who doesn't give a shit about his 'family' I mean – look at you, your touch, it's like ice and in your eyes is the look of resentment. I can sense it, and I don't like it."

"Son-" William began but was cut short as with sheer anger Andrew walked up to him. "Don't you dare call me that!"

William nodded. "Andrew what do you want me to say? You want me to say I'm sorry? Well I'm not OK! Yeah, so I walked out on you and your brother, I walked out for a reason

– you see your mum was ill, yes, but she was making Zach ill too. Speaking of which, where is your brother?"

Andrew folded his arms across his chest, he huffed and puffed. "Zach left the house in December last year, he needed to get away from Mum, I chose to stay because Mum is all I had, 'cause you left me!"

William shifted his weight from his left leg to his right leg. "So where is Zach now?"

Andrew grew angry with every question fired at him. "How the fuck should I know – I'm not his keeper!"

"Andrew stop the swearing!" William shouted at him. People passed by the father and son reunion, just staring at them, not saying anything. "You know what Andrew? Go home to your mum and Ill come and visit you. We will have a talk later this week OK?"

William began walking back home when Andrew shouted at him. "Well William I would go back to my dear mum, but you know what? I can't do that, you know why?"

William turned round. "Why?" He wasn't expecting what he was about to hear.

Andrew smiled. "Because the bitch is dead!"

William went white with shock. "What do you mean she's dead?"

Andrew cocked his head to one side. "Because I killed her Dad! I killed her because you left me with that thing I used to call my mum. That thing that abused me: sexually, physically and mentally. You know what Dad?" he said sarcastically. "She took me out of school and the school board allowed it! She took me out, promising them she would home school me and guess what? Oh I got home schooled, I got home schooled good, put it this way for me being twelve I know the inside and outside of a woman's body. I know biology especially!"

William didn't know what to say, he stood there in shock and awe.

What did he just hear?

Was it true?

He didn't know what to do. Before he could come to his senses, Andrew had turned and walked away back up Bearsden Road, leaving him standing there in shock.

But that was the least of William Light's worries for now.

39
I Just Want to be Famous
29th August 2000

He stared into the mirror above the sink in his flat. "I can almost taste it," he whispered through clenched teeth. "This shit makes no sense to me. What does it all mean?"

Then the voice answered him. "You can almost save it. All this shit makes no sense at the moment, but it will mean everything you wanted: the taste, the touch, the lime-light!"

"Yeah, I can't stop now," he began, "this may be the last chance I get to be famous!"

The voice chimed in, "You've dreamed of trading places. But I have made you change your face. You can fill the shoes of every sadistic serial killer to ever be born. There is no time to lose."

He nodded and smiled at his reflection - the reflection of his inner demons, the 'ones' that tell him what to do. "I just want to be famous!"

The voices understood him, but reassured him. "Just be careful what you wish for."

He walked into the living room and sat down across from the

TV. The TV wasn't switched on, so he still saw his reflection of his inner demon. "I stuck my dick in this game like a rapist and I promised to you I would seek my revenge. You have guided through this and I'm thankful for that."

The voices agreed with him. "Zach I'm pissed off - you've got to murder more, murder someone else and make it gory, gory as hell!"

He nodded in acceptance to the voice. "I want to be like a gangster, you know – I want people to shit their pants when they see me as if I'm waving a chainsaw above my head."

The voice listened and then instructed, "When you kill again, you want to show them pain as though you were the thumb tack they slept on, son. You should scream attack as though you just stepped on one! And nobody will fuck with you, you'll be like a zombie with the rigamortis setting in and you won't be dying of boredom any longer."

He nodded again. "Yeah – I'll be screaming, 'you going to fuck with a guy who licks the blades of his chainsaws!' and they will just be more terrified than ever!"

The voices laughed. "You're almost famous, a few more bodies before you hit your intended targets and then you'll be famous."

He gave off an evil cackle, almost like a witch's laugh. "I'm back for revenge; I lost a battle that ain't going to be happening again. I'll pull out all the stops, I'll be the new Michael Myers, and I would tell that old psycho to pass the torch to this whacko before I take a shit in his Jack-O-Lantern and smash it on his porch!"

The voice laughed back at him. "They'll call you the champ, the space shuttle destroyer. I think it would be awesome if you took a belt or a neck tie and wrapped it around two people's throats while they are having sex – just so you can shout, 'they can go fuck themselves and just die!' You can do this Zach, because I know you ain't looking back, only forward, you'll hit it and make it, you'll finally be famous!"

It was time once again for the whole world to know that Zach was back again.

40
The Media
30th August 2000

Police lights flickered, cameras flashed, reporters all yelled question after question to the Chief of police.

Alex Grimm stood on the steps of the Clydebank town hall in front of a podium which housed microphones from different television networks: BBC, STV and Sky News. Alongside the television networks microphones were also housed from various newspapers – *Daily Record*, *The Sun*, *The Herald*, and *The Evening Times*. Everyone wanted to know what was going on and what the police were doing.

"I am standing outside Clydebank's town hall where the Chief of police is informing us about the tragedy that has befallen this small town, which is rich in history," Thomas Marshall a twenty-three year old news reporter working for Sky News said into the camera. "It has been made official that a serial killer is on the loose in Clydebank, and between January and August 19th three bodies have been found murdered in cold blood. Firstly an old woman robbed of her money and stabbed viciously and left to rot in a path. Secondly a young teenager, out having a laugh with her friends in the local bar, stabbed and ripped apart by a wine bottle. Then the case of the young girl found in her bed, beaten and stabbed to death with then her kidney removed and half sent to an officer at the police station with a letter claiming that the other half was eaten by the killer. The Clydebank police force are continuing to working on the case and are asking for any information from the public on the nights in question when the murders had taking place. They have set up an incident number that people can call if they have any information; the number to call is a free phone number – 0800-225-999. Viewers will find the number at the bottom of the screen and on our website at skynews.com. People have dubbed the killer, the modern day Jack the Ripper due to the letter and half a kidney that was sent to one police officer in particular, his name was Officer William Light. Mr Light has refused any comments as of yet, as the case still ongoing. I am Thomas Marshall reporting live from Clydebank near Glasgow, now back to the studio."

As Thomas finished his news report, he walked over to the news van and with his cameraman, packed everything up. "Listen Kenny before we head off, I'm going to go get something to eat. Do you want anything?"

Kenny shook his head. "No mate, I'll just pack everything up and wait here in the van." Thomas nodded and walked away down Dumbarton Road towards the shopping centre. He crossed the road and headed up passed Singers Bar and followed the signs for the shopping centre. He walked past where the teenage girl was found murdered in the dark path, just behind the council offices. Cutting across the council offices car park he followed the pathway around to the Forth and Clyde Canal and just as he passed under the tunnel running underneath Kilbowie Road, that's when he noticed it.

It floated in the murky water of the canal; Thomas looked at it with a puzzled and a horrified look on his face. What he was looking at was indeed another body, by the looks of it a man, an old man was lying face down tangled in crisp packets and weeds. Floating down the canal towards a packed shopping centre, where kids would see the bloated body.

As Thomas reached for his mobile phone, he noticed something else floating nearby: wet hair covered the body and it floated aimlessly down with the man's now decaying body. Thomas felt bile rise into his throat and couldn't control it as the remains of the morning's breakfast came up out of his mouth, like a spray of water onto the pebbled pathway. After wiping his mouth, Thomas pulled out his mobile phone and dialled the cameraman back down at the town hall.

It rang and rang and then Kenny picked up. "Hello Tommy what's up?"

Thomas cleared his throat. "Kenny, get the police to come up to the canal just at the tunnel at the council offices – there's two dead bodies in the water."

Kenny dropped his phone and ran over to a few police officers. "Excuse me officers – I've just got a call from my reporter. He's up at the tunnel at the canal across from the council offices. He says he has discovered two bodies."

The officers broke apart and one went over to the Chief and the other spoke into his radio. Reactions followed and police started to move to their cars. Alex Grimm went white with shock and raced to his car.

From across the street, outside the Singers Bar, he sat watching the movie he had literally made. The horror movie, the true story. The voices laughed and he laughed along with them. He sipped from his beer bottle and then laughed loudly.

He was almost famous before, but now he knew he was going to more famous than Jack the Ripper himself.

41
The Discovery of Sarah Light
4th May 2000

Broughton Road in Summerston just off Maryhill, was a quiet street, houses with well kept gardens lined the entire street. Coming up the left hand-side across from Broughton Road stood Lambhill Cemetery, a graveyard spanning over various acres. It stood out especially at night, eerie gravestones staring out over the street and surrounding areas.

Just next to a Royal Mail post box stood number 64 Broughton Road - home of the Light family. William Light stepped out of his police car as other police cars came to a halt, stopping any traffic coming up or going down the road. Police lights flickered in the night sky as various officers started walking up the driveway towards the front door of William Light's former family home.

William didn't think he would ever be back at this house, especially in these circumstances. As soon as his young son Andrew told him that he killed his mother and buried her in the back garden he ran back home and dived into his car and raced to Clydebank Police station. He raced into the station, told the desk sergeant to arrange police officers from the office and Maryhill police station to go to the house.

He raced into the Chief's office and told Alex the whole story. Alex agreed to get officers out there.

William looked up at his old family home. To him it looked all dark and dreary now, not the once happy place that he shared with his wife and two sons. Now ten years later he stood waiting on the go ahead to enter the premises to *apparently* find his ex-wife dead and buried, *apparently* murdered by his youngest son.

"William," a fellow police officer began, "you stay here mate, we will check it out first and then you can come in. OK?"

William shook his head. "No, no need to. I left this house in 1990; I won't feel anything if we discover what he told me."

The police officer nodded and firstly he chapped on the front door, three times, but no-one answered. Then he called for the 'battering ram' and the officers carrying it came forward and broke the door open.

They all entered the house and were immediately thrown back by the smell and look of the place. A few officers went back outside for some fresh air while William stood in the living room amongst empty vodka bottles, beer cans, and empty take-away containers, and that's when he saw the note on the dust covered table. He bent down and read it. It said:

Dear Dad,

As a kid I looked up to you, you were my hero. Now the only thing I never see enough of you. The last thing I said to you was 'no I'm staying', I loved you and now it's too late to say to you. Just didn't know what to do or how to deal with it, even now deep down I'm still livid. To think, I used to blame me, it was you that walked out on us. YOU that left us with her. I was young then and you still left. I wondered what I did to you to make you hate me. I hope you die Dad. I'll even help you on your way. See you real soon Dad - I promise'

Your son,
Andrew.

Next to that note, lay another letter; folded up it read:

You don't know how much I want to watch your skin burn. All melted on the floor. Tell me sixty times it was nothing please. Come to me in guilt I promise it won't go unpaid dear mother, its okay just lay down on a million scorpions. Let me hear you scream as they sting. I can't bring myself to leave you, no matter how bad I want to. I wish just once that you could go die in a moment so I don't have to. I am not heartless but my heart doesn't beat no more. I would love to put you in a pool and hold you down till your last breath is filled with water. I hate you so much Mum, but to hurt you would kill me. I want to slowly run a knife and make blood pour out of you, all over my hand. I wish I could just take a bath with you then get out, throwing a hair dryer in the water, watching your body is so electric ha-ha please more like pathetic. I love you but honestly I don't. You my dear mother I wouldn't hurt you. Drink your poisoned vodka and slowly sleep forever. I hate you Mum, but I love you. Go to sleep Mum, please forever.

Your son

Andrew

William stood back up and gulped trying to get some saliva back into his dry mouth.

"William, you alright?" another officer asked from behind him.

William nodded and started looking round the place.

The place, by the looks of it, hadn't been cleaned in years. William followed by two officers, with strong stomachs, walked through the grime.

"You take upstairs." William pointed to the younger officer of the two. "Look for any signs of life." The officer nodded and climbed the stairs. William turned to the older officer of the two. "You take the living room, dining room and kitchen and I'll round up the rest of the squad and take the garden." The older officer nodded and walked around the living room, moving discarded vodka bottles out the way so he could look for any living thing.

William moved through to the kitchen and turned the lock in the back door, he walked out and immediately noticed disturbed earth to the right of the garden - there was a shade of grass area that was just mud, it had no grass on it.

He radioed for other officers to come out to the back garden and agreed with them that they would need forensics and digging equipment.

One hour later, the white forensic tent was up over the crime-scene. Police blocked the road leading up to Broughton Road. No one was to get through or be able to leave their houses.

Crime-scene investigators piled through the house, looking for any bit of evidence.

When they uncovered the remains of Sandra Light (which

was identified by her former husband William) a few police officers brought up last night's dinner on the grass surrounding the body.

The body was headless, but the head was near the body. The corpse wore only her nightdress which was covered in blood, although it was mixed with dirt and mud, earthworms and other insects crawled over the body. The leading forensics investigator gave a time of death which matched what William was told by his youngest son.

William was questioned in depth as to why his youngest son would kill his mother. But William didn't have any answers.

When police searched the house various sexual toys were found along with x-rated material, including photos of Andrew naked. Detectives decided that this was the motive. William was questioned again as of where Andrew would go. But William had no idea, he only just seen his son after a ten year absence.

The media was alerted and a police e-fit was put out to catch Andrew Light. William did mention that he could possibly be away looking for his brother Zach, who has left the house in December 1999 as Andrew had said. But the whereabouts of Zach was a mystery as well.

Back in Clydebank, Zach watched the news unfold on TV, they named the victim found in the garden as Sandra Light and showed the house where she was found. Zach grew angry as he was the one with the plan, he was the one who was going to kill his mother after he had murdered his father. Then the photo and name flashed up on screen:

"Police are looking for a teenager by the name Andrew Light. He is wanted in connection with the death of Sandra Light. Police have also released that Andrew was last seen on Bearsden Road leading onto Kinfauns Drive in Drumchapel. If you see this boy, please contact your local police office as soon as possible."

Zach went white with fright; his younger brother had killed their mum. Ironically he was the one that wanted to stay with her, and now he is wanted for the murder.

Although Zach felt sick, he also cherished the fact that at least one parent was now dead.

42
Newsflash
30th August 2000

The canal pathway was cordoned off by police tape. Media again swarmed the main road of Clydebank, which overlooked the canal that ran through Clydebank.

Media crews and the some public members stood in the council offices car park watching the proceedings. Police kept them at bay from the crime-scene.

Thomas Marshall stood giving a statement.

Zach Light stood smiling in the crowd.

Police divers waded through the waters of the canal to retrieve the bodies of a human and an animal. They pulled the bodies onto the grass verge surrounding the canal, forensics gathered and gave their verdict to the Alex Grimm. Alex nodded and walked over to his long time friend and fellow police officer William.

"William," he began, "it's the same MO again. We have to find Andrew and find him soon. This thing is big, the media have got a hold of this, and they have linked you and Andrew together. It's only a matter of time."

William bowed his head. "What do you want me to do Alex? I can't magically find Andrew. I know he's the number one suspect now, but I don't think it was him – I don't think it is him who is killing these people!"

Alex breathed deeply. "William, you saw your ex-wife's body and he confessed to you that he killed her, what makes you think he hasn't killed the rest?"

"I don't know," William began, "I just know that's all. Andrew was a good boy, hell both my sons were good boys, it was just their mother who was messed up!"

"I'm taking you off the case," Alex told a worried William.

"What!?" William yelled, startling everyone around them. "You can't do this Alex!"

"I believe I can and I just have," Alex told him. "It's not a request Bill it's an order. I believe I can and I just have," Alex told him. "You've got some holidays to take, so why don't you go home and just take a break? Take Nancy and your little girl away from here for a while."

William shook his head in disgust, but did as he was told and walked away over to his car. He got in and pulled away from the crime scene. He was now off the case.

"Chief Inspector," a voice shouted from the crowd of media perched on the road above the canal.

Alex looked up. "Yeah?"

The person that shouted walked down and towards Alex. "Hi, it's James Speed from BBC news. So is it Andrew Light who you are looking for with regards to the murders surrounding Clydebank?"

Alex shook his head. "No comment at this time, thank you." Alex walked back over to the canal, but on his way he turned to another officer, "Get those fucking vultures away from here please!"

The officer nodded and grabbed a few other officers to move the media away.

Zach looked on as the camera crew from all media stations were moved on, he overheard the BBC reporter state again that this was the work of his young brother Andrew, his hands tightened, his face began to go a nice shade of red and the voices began to talk again.

The voice of a woman spoke to him, "Zach, you have to move to a different location now your dad is off the case." The voice sounded awfully like his mother talking to him.

"Where do I go now though?" he whispered back to the voice.

"The Bluebell Woods Zach; move your location to Drumchapel, show them what hell is like!"

Zach smiled.

Drumchapel was the hometown of his father, and was about to become a hometown of bloodshed.

43
Murder, it Catches Up on All of Us
19th August 2000

Cruising down the M8 heading out of Glasgow, Jacob Kane and his baby daughter Rebecca headed away from the pain, the horror of what he had actually done.

Going at a nice steady speed, nice drive down the motorway until his back tyre burst. Knowing that he didn't have a spare, and if he stopped police would question him and discover who he was, he continued driving but way below the speed limit. He began to smell burning rubber and looked in his side mirror, flames were coming from the burst tyre, but nothing was going to stop Jacob from leaving Scotland once and for all.

Jacob looked into the rear-view mirror and watched his baby girl sitting blowing raspberries in the back seat. "Hey baby, you know daddy loves you don't you?"

Rebecca smiled and giggled at her daddy. Then Jacob saw the blue flashing lights in the rear-view mirror.

The police had finally caught up with him. He pulled over into the side and the police stopped behind him, lights still flashing.

Jacob looked into the rear-view mirror again. "Just stay quiet baby girl and let Daddy deal with this man."

A dark shadow cast over the driver's window and a knock on the window came next.

"Just stay calm Kane, nice and calm – no need to get worked up," Jacob told himself. He rolled down the window.

"Sir," the traffic police officer began, "you have been driving with a burnt out tyre, are you aware of that?"

"I just noticed Officer," Jacob began, "I was trying to get off the motorway so I could check it."

The officer nodded. "Why didn't you just pull over and sort it sooner?"

"Because Officer," Jacob began, "I don't have a spare tyre in the car, and with my daughter in the back, I didn't want her to get upset with all the traffic driving at some speed passed us on here."

The officer tsk-tsked him. "Sir, it's even worse driving with a blown out tyre with a child in back, what if you lost control and crashed?"

Jacob smiled. "Officer I never lose control, I'm always in control!"

"Can I see your licence and registration please?" the officer asked.

"I don't have it on me," Jacob lied. Of course he had it on him, but he couldn't show the officer it or they would take him in for questioning. "This is my mum's car and my papers are in my car."

"So you are driving with your daughter in a car that has a blown tyre and you don't have your papers with you?" the officer questioned. Jacob nodded. "Sir, can you step out of the car please."

"What for?" Jacob began. "I haven't done anything illegal have I?"

"To an extent – yes you have," the officer replied, "but for you and your daughter's own safety I'll take you back to the station and get your car picked up."

"But all I need is a new tyre," Jacob began to get anxious. "Surely you can radio for an AA truck to help me out? I'm not with them but I can pay them in cash!"

"Sir please," the officer began again, "just step out of the car, bring your daughter and we will get this sorted."

Jacob sighed and then nodded in defeat. "OK, give me a second."

The officer stood back. "I need to know your name Sir."

Jacob mumbled his name.

"Sorry Sir, what was that?"

Jacob climbed out of his car. "My name is Jacob Kane."

The officer nodded. "Thank you, now you grab your daughter and I'll meet you back at the car. Please mind and lock your car up, and please put on your hazards." The officer walked back to his squad car and Jacob noticed him speaking into the radio. Jacob quickly scooped up Rebecca and locked the car securely and walked fast to the officer's car. "OK officer, all done."

The officer nodded and opened the back door for him and his daughter. Jacob placed Rebecca in and secured her with the seatbelt and then climbed in himself. The officer got in front, started up the engine and pulled back onto the motorway and headed towards the police station.

On route, the officer picked up his radio. "Control this is 257 over."

The radio crackled. "257 go ahead over."

"I am on route back to the police station with a man and his daughter. Their car blew out a tyre, for safety reasons bringing them back to station, over."

"Understood 257, what is the gentleman's name? Over." control asked.

"His name is Jacob Kane, over" the officer stated.

Jacob Kane looked up from attending to his daughter at the sound of his name getting mentioned. The radio was silent for what felt like a long time. Then control kicked in. "257, Jacob Kane is supposedly dead, are you sure that you have the right name? Over."

Before the officer could answer, Jacob leaned over and with one quick move, grabbed the officer's head and forcefully banged it against the steering wheel. The car swerved to the left and to the right. Rebecca began to cry, but Jacob stayed calm and pushed the officer over to the passenger's seat. The car sped up but Jacob climbed over and into the driver's seat and brought it under control.

Control came over the radio again. "257 this is control did you get my last message? Over."

Jacob looked at the radio and pondered what he should do next.

Should he answer it?

Or just leave it?

He picked up the handset. "Control this is 257, the gentleman in question is not, I repeat, is not Jacob Kane. I got his name wrong, his name is James McCain. Over."

Jacob steadied the car and tried to soothe Rebecca to a minimum noise.

Control crackled in again. "257 is everything OK? I hear the baby crying? Over."

Jacob got frustrated. "Yes control, everything is OK. Arrival time forty minutes. Over and out."

They turned off a junction and headed back towards Glasgow.

He looked in the rear-view at Rebecca and told her, "You mean the world to me honey. I love you." The officer began to stir as they entered Whiteinch.

Whiteinch was a district of Partick in Glasgow and was home to 'Fossil Grove' - a centre that housed fossilised trees and plants. It sat in a public park called Victoria Park.

Jacob stopped the car near the entrance of the park, it was now getting very dark and barely no-one was about. The officer was still unconscious as Jacob got out the car, Rebecca was now fast asleep and Jacob had turned off the radio – he had thrown the officer's own radio out of the car while driving. He went round and opened up the passenger door, leaving Rebecca in the back seat in the car; he scooped up the officer and carried him over to the park.

Victoria Park had insufficient lights to light the pathways around the pond in the centre of the park and Jacob carried the officer up and over to the place that housed the fossilized remains of ancient trees. He dropped the officer onto the grass verge and picked up a bolder that lay near the doorway. Jacob noticed there was no alarm on the door, (good old Glasgow security) just a simple padlock, that he bashed open with the bolder. He pulled the door opened and then proceeded to pick up the officer again. He entered and closed the door behind him.

Victoria Park was a lovely landscaped area that was designed to commemorate the Jubilee of Queen Victoria. A nice clean place to 'get rid' of someone that knows about him. Jacob threw the unconscious officer over the railing and he landed with a hard thump on the fossilised exhibition. The officer began to come around as Jacob climbed over the railing and stood above his prey.

The officer blinked and then opened his eyes fully and began looking around, adjusting to the small light and his surroundings. "Where – where have you taken me?"

Jacob only smiled, a sly evil smile. "Listen no chit-chat, let's just get to the main point, you know who I am and well I got to get rid of people that knows me. You see I want to make a fresh start with my baby girl and the only way to do that is to get away from Glasgow!"

The officer looked worried. "Listen, just calm down. I don't know who you are or indeed what you've done, just please don't do anything stupid."

Jacob cocked his head to one side. "Did you just call me stupid? Listen I am anything but stupid, do you know why? Cause I got away with it! I got away with killing my wife, her lover and his kid, and do you know what? I fucking loved it! I even faked my own suicide and I was so close to getting away from this fucking place, until you came along and put a spanner in my works!"

"So...so you are Jacob Kane?" the officer began. "And you're telling me that you faked your death to get away with murder? Listen, please don't do anything rash."

"Rash?" Jacob responded. "Rash? I'm not going to do anything rash – I'm just going to kill you! Yeah so I killed my wife and her lover and his kid. Later on I slit my mother's throat - you got a problem with that? Didn't think so! Do you know the Kilpatrick Hills? Well, that's where I took my wife and murdered her, took her there and slit her throat, and then I dragged her sorry ass back home and displayed her corpse as though someone broke in. Great plan don't you think? Well, answer me you asshole! I'm a serial killer so what? What you going to do? Put me in prison? Oh I'm so scared; I'm shaking in my boots! Ill be out in thirty years - human rights, you gotta love the European Union law. Brussels I applaud you!"

The officer stared at him, just listening to him probably made him shit himself. And Jacob loved it, loved every moment of it.

"You see officer I would have continued killing, but I had to get out away from this place, I mean let's face it, Glasgow has got a lot more to worry about right now than me. I had to get my baby girl and leave here, once and for all. Tell me this; if my tyre didn't blow out tonight, would you and your police force know I was still alive? No - exactly just as I thought! You are a fud, Strathclyde's police force are idiots, hell where's Taggart when you need him? Oh sorry that's fiction isn't it? And this my friend is very much real. I am the real deal, the devil that walks among you pathetic human beings. I am the resurrection and the light. Oh wait, that idiot carpenter already claimed that didn't he? Well fuck heaven, fuck God and fuck Jesus Christ! Cause you know what? You should be worshipping me! That's right – me! And since you personally don't, I'll make you worship me. Now how would you like your skin to be hemmed up in good old Scottish kilts?"

The officer began to squirm but didn't dare stand up.

"Now now don't struggle officer, you know this is for the best. It was either going to be in prison - which by the way would be great, or it was dying. I prefer the latter one. So officer have you got anything to say?" Jacob spoke nice and politely to the scared individual.

The officer squirmed even more but still didn't dare stand up.

Jacob picked up the scared man and proceeded to tie a rope he had found discarded outside around the officer's neck.

"Please...please don't do this!" the officer pleaded. A warm stream of urine poured down the inside of his leg.

Jacob tied the officer's hands and then pushed him back down on the floor then tied his feet.

"I learned a lot from the master!" Jacob exclaimed. He then threw the remainder of the rope up over the railing and climbed up, he pulled the officer in the restraints up so he was in a hanging position. He swung back and forth as Jacob climbed back down and stared at him, Jacob then pulled out a knife and raised it to the terrified officer. He cut deep into his groin and slit him from groin to sterna. Blood flowed onto the fossilised ground below their feet. And then he began cutting and peeling his skin off of his dead body (well, he wouldn't need it anymore). He would now get away with a fifth murder, much more than his 'saviour' Zach Light.

The stories this will make in the media, a police officer dead and found in Fossil Grove: skinned and left hanging.

Jacob stepped back and looked at the dead officer. He cocked his head to one side. "You know officer – I love my daughter more than anything. Now I know you are probably thinking – what if Rebecca, once she's older finds out I killed her mum and grandma? Well that isn't going to happen. You see officer I have a plan, a plan that will take the blame off of me and directly onto someone far worse than me. I'll get away with murder so to speak and this other guy will take the fall, I guarantee it! But fuck it, it's over, there's no more reason to cry no more I got my baby, baby the only lady that I adore, and that is Rebecca. So sayonara officer, it was nice to know you. My baby's travelled back to the arms of her rightful owner and suddenly it seems that my shoulder blades have just shifted it's like the greatest gift you can get the weight has been lifted."

Jacob left the officer hanging and climbed back over the railing. He stood admiring his work and then placed the skin on the viewing platform over the fossils, he bent down and with the knife he sliced words into the skin, after he had finished he stood up and left.

The words he ripped into the officer's skin were:

DO YOU SEE THE LIGHT, OFFICER WILLIAM LIGHT?

Jacob walked out of fossil grove and back down the pathway

towards the police car. Rebecca was still fast asleep as he opened up the back door and pulled her out. He carried his daughter onto Dumbarton Road and waited for the bus into town; according to the timetable one would be along shortly.

Jacob whispered into his daughter's ear, "Daddy's here. And I am not going anywhere, baby I love you!"

The number 62 First Bus service pulled up, Jacob climbed aboard and paid the fare, he sat down at the front of the bus with Rebecca still cuddling him and smiled.

44
The Bluebells are Now Red
2nd September 2000

A moon lit sky is interrupted by the sounds of a scream. Bats and birds fly from the twisted perch that is the old walnut tree. Its branches reach in to the inky abyss in search of the cold air. A second scream breaks the silence once more.

A girl runs through the branches. Little fingers poke at her legs while she tries to navigate the foliage. She works towards a clearing as heavy footsteps pound behind her. Hating herself for taking a short path, she fights the urge to sneak a second peek of her pursuer. She hoped that he would leave her alone long enough to make a break.

Steam rolled from the lips of the large man as he positioned himself in the moonlight. He stared at his prey. Another deep breath flew in to the night air. Cold leather and rubber worked their way through the mud as he stayed on her path. The smell of perfume and sweat intoxicated the man. He hungered for the moment when he would rip her arms off and have the release from the blood rolling down his flesh. A smile broke his steel like exterior. He knew that the more that she ran, the brighter the blood would be that flowed through her veins.

The girl darted in to the clearing. Twenty feet until she reached the road. "Leave me alone," she cried to the man that followed. She just needed to punch through the mud and then it was back to civilization. She could hide in her room for the next thirty years and hope that he wouldn't find her. *Wishful thinking*, she thought. Rain, which seeped from a passing cloud, caused the mud to turn to quick sand. With each step, she sunk deeper and deeper in to the mud below.

More steam poured from the mangled lips. He let out a light grunt as he came to the clearing. He could smell the girl as she fought her way through the mud. A mental map popped up in his mind, and he laid out a route to the street. The machete made an ominous 'ting' as it came out of the leather sheathe. He navigated his route to the edge of the wood. He squatted and waited as the girl fought a little more.

She smelt the asphalt of the road. She could almost hear a car off in the distance. She saw her freedom. A twig snapped. She picked up her feet. She felt the ground as she approached a small tree line. Her damp shirt seemed to soak up the night air. A chill rolled down her spine. "What do you want from me?" The cries in the night are useless; however there was something about it that seemed to calm her nerves. Air settled around her as her heart pounded in her chest. The world grew silent. A cricket chirped in the distance. She ran through the mud to the street.

"Fuck," he said. A wave of other voices made themselves known.

"You do know that you needed to kill her," the first said. It was the voice of an older woman. He always thought that this was his mother coming to make things right. She had a way of making everything right. Plus this 'mother' was better than his real mother.

"Why did you let her go?" the second asked. This was the informed voice. Intelligent in speech, he came to call this one Alfred.

The last one that he waited for took longer to speak. He focused on this one the most. It was an inner child that seemed to have the best grip on reality. "Zach, you should have killed her when you had the chance. Now, she's going to get the authorities and they are going to kill you. Did you miss the feeling of having all of that wonderful gooeyness run all over your body?" The voice trailed off as Zach watched the girl make it to the street.

Freedom, is what the girl thought. She knew that the monster was still waiting for her. She took off away from the short tree line. Her feet warmed as she ran faster away from the place. A pain started in her back. She thought it was a spasm from running, but then it moved to her chest. She looked down. Moonlight, mixed with a thin coat of blood, reflected off of the blade. A thick thud was the last thing that she heard.

He had come to Drumchapel for a change of scenery, and the scenery will run red with the blood of more victims.

45
Looking for Andrew
10th May 2000

The briefing room was crowded from pillar to post with every officer from two divisions of Strathclyde police, half from Maryhill police force and the rest from Clydebank police force.

The subject – the search for Andrew Light. This time only Alex Grimm stood in front of the task force, no William Light in sight.

"We are looking for a young teenager, answers to the name of Andrew Light. He is wanted for the murder of his mother Sandra Light, and is a suspect in the murders that have taken place here in Clydebank since January this year." Grimm passed out a detailed description of the boy, of his best friend's son. The police officers took a leaflet each and passed it on, mumbling under the breaths to each other. Alex heard William getting mentioned, along with his other son Zach. He also heard talk amongst the room that William was suspended, and rumours that he was taken off the case altogether.

"Listen up people!" Alex yelled. "Nobody has sighted

Andrew since he confronted his father a few weeks ago. So put the word out to every member of the public, inform them that if approached by this boy – cause let's face it that's all he is – then seek help as soon as, Andrew could be armed, and as we have seen could very well be dangerous. That's all just now, so guys keep your eyes peeled and stay safe."

The officers got up out of their chairs and began disbanding, leaving the station to hunt for Andrew.

The officers poured out of the police station: some got into their cars, while some began walking to various parts of the town.

Andrew stood under a tree to the side of the station watching everyone leave, he stood in the shadows, with his hood up so no one could recognise him. He wasn't planning on killing anyone else, but heard through discarded newspapers that the police were claiming he was a suspect in the killings that were happening in Clydebank. He felt let down by this; he only killed his mother for the amount of abuse she did to him. He told his father because he needed help, and what does his father do? Go and get more officers to hunt him down like a dog. Andrew bowed his head, turned and walked away, away to go get his brother. He spoke to a few people on the streets who pinpointed where Zach was staying, so he made his way to the flats.

It was time to finally be reunited with his older brother, five months after he walked out of the family home. Andrew kept wondering if his brother had seen the news, had seen the papers, he wondered if his brother knew he was wanted for the murder of their mum. Although, he did know Zach would be happy that the bitch was dead finally!

He would find out soon, if his brother was to help him evade the police.

46
Voices Distract Him Again
7th September 2000

He kept running, running away from the shadow, that's what he'd come to call it. He thought it was a figment of his imagination. Something that wasn't really there, but low and behold there it was; it followed him everywhere, reflecting off metal. He could see it, and it could see him. It always glared at him with those dark eyes. Eyes he called 'the devils eyes'. But it wasn't the devil that he was sure of. The devil is nothing like this - this thing.

He kept running and running, but no matter where he ran to, it was there: watching, waiting, waiting for him, and waiting to take him.

"Run, run little man, run away fast," he heard it snarl.

"Go away, annoy someone else - please!" he yelled back.

It laughed with such evil in its voice. "You don't know who I am, do you?"

He shook his head. "No please just leave me alone!"

It smiled back at him, looking directly in his eyes. 'I'm you!'

At that point he raised his fist and smashed the mirror, and it vanished.

The voices were taking over his body, he knew he was out of control. Zach Light no longer existed, the voices were controlling his body as though he was a robot, and he was the man killing people but being controlled by a darker force.

His main aim was to kill his mother and father but that all changed the night his younger brother found him back in May. That night changed everything, not for the good but for the bad. Andrew sought help from him, and at first he consoled his young sibling, until the darker force invaded him.

He still has nightmares about that night, but he knew he couldn't control the darkness inside him anymore, he knew it was nearly over. His revenge was close to being carried out. Soon the game would come full circle; he had to oblige what the voices wanted him to do. So far he had killed four women, a man and his dog and then again that night in May when he was confronted by his brother and heard what he had done to their mother.

Now it was September, but the voices wanted him to continue killing a few more before getting to his dear old daddy. His mother had been taken care of by Andrew, so it was just dad to go. The voices controlled his body like a puppet and he listened to the voices.

Another murder was due for Drumchapel.

47
Brothers Reunited
10th May 2000 - Night

He rocked back and forward on the couch - he did it, he finally did. But it wasn't him that did it; it was the voices they made him do it.

He killed his brother. The brother he left behind to live with that abusive woman they called a mother. He killed his young brother.

For what?

That was a question he kept repeating to himself over and over again, beating the sides of his head with both fists. "Why did you make me kill him?" he screamed to the voices. "Why my brother?" Then he cried, tears streaming down his face, resulting in a small puddle forming on his lap.

"Zach," the woman's voice began in his head. "Zach, he killed your mother – that was your duty. That was your task and he took it away from you. Plus you put him out of his misery: he was abused by your mother, sexually, physically and mentally so you put him out of his misery!"

"No, no, NO!" he screamed. "He was my young brother. I

didn't have to kill him, not like that!"

Then the other voice screamed at him, this time it sounded like an older man. "Zach stop bubbling, stand up and be a man; this wasn't your first time. And you enjoyed it; tell the truth it felt good!"

"He was my BROTHER!" he screamed, banging the sides of his head again with both fists.

One hour prior to him screaming at the voices in his head, he was disturbed by a knock at his front door. Usually he didn't answer the door unless he was expecting someone, but he was intrigued to see who was there. He peered through the peep-hole and saw that it was his younger brother, Andrew, standing there, looking a little worse for wear. He opened the door and ushered his brother in and closed the door behind him, locking and chaining it. He ushered Andrew into the living room informing him to excuse the mess - because let's face it, it wasn't exactly a palace now was it!

It had been months since they both saw each other and now Andrew had found him. He told Andrew to sit down and while doing so retrieved two bottles of Budweiser from the fridge. He handed his wee brother one - yeah so he was young, what's going to happen? Their parents aren't going to do anything – especially mother!

Andrew took the beer and took a swig of it. "So Zach how you been?"

Weird question to start off with... He thought to himself, but he went along with it. "Fine."

"I guess you saw on the news what I did?" Andrew asked, sitting back on the sofa.

He nodded and swigged from his beer bottle. "Yes."

"I had to do it Zach," Andrew began, "that bitch abused me! She used me as a sex toy, took pictures of me in various poses! Wouldn't let me out the house. But I won! I coaxed her down into the kitchen with a bottle of vodka and bam!" he slammed his fists together. "I hit her over the head with a shovel. Then I buried her in the back garden, but what happens next? Lo and behold the bitch is still alive, she started stirring so I jumped in the hole and took her head clean off with the shovel!"

Zach took a swig from his beer again and finished it, he stood up. "Want another?" Andrew nodded and he went back into the kitchen.

Andrew was still telling him how he killed their mother and went on to say about the police wanting him for the murders in Clydebank.

He stood at the fridge, just left of the kitchen door. He opened it up and then he heard her:

"Zach," the voice called. It sounded far away. "Zach it's me, your mother." He raised both hands to his head. He still heard Andrew continue to rabbit on about the murders and why they wanted him - a mere twelve year old - surely the police force knew it couldn't be him?

"Zach," the voice called, "listen to me, listen to your mother!" He shook his head, banging his fists against his temples. "You know you have to kill him, don't you Zach? You have to avenge my murder!"

"I was going to kill you myself!" Zach whispered through gritted teeth to the voice.

"Yes and he got there before you, didn't he?" the voice told him. "Now go be good boy and kill the little shit!"

He shook his head. "No – no, NO!" he told the voice, through gritted teeth and the taste of his own blood.

"You know what Zach?" the voice began. "You are just like your father!"

He shot his head up and breathed heavily. "What do you want me to do Mum?"

"Poison him," the voice told him.

"Yes Zach, poison him, then cut him up badly!" another voice spoke - an elder man this time.

Zach nodded, he bent down to under the sink and pulled out

some ant killer, he opened up the container and poured some beer down the sink and topped it up with the insecticide.

"Stick a few amphetamine tablets in it too, remember and crush them first," the female voice told him.

He nodded and smiled.

"Bro, where's that beer?" Andrew called from the living room.

He came through and handed him the bad concoction. "Finally," Andrew said, taking the beer from his big brother. "What the hell were you doing in there? Talking to someone?"

Zach looked a bit worried. "Just myself, I couldn't open the damn bottles," he laughed; a simple laugh but a fake one at that. He sat down next to his brother and watched as he began to drink from the bottle of poison.

After just a few sips, Andrew began to feel a burning sensation: he dropped the bottle, put both hands up to his throat and began clawing and scratching at it as though his throat was on fire. (Well it was after all!) "Something's wrong with the beer Bro!" he managed to say.

Zach just took another swig of his beer and placed it on the table. He stood up and went into the kitchen again; he pulled open the kitchen drawer and pulled out a carving knife. He turned and watched as his younger brother tried to stand up.

"I...I don't feel too good!" Andrew declared. He began swaying and then puking up a foam-like substance followed by blood. So the poison began working.

Zach smiled as he marched up to his young brother and stood in front of him. He cocked his head to the left and then to the right.

"Tell him Zach; tell him you are the killer of Clydebank - the Clydebank Ripper! Tell him!" the voice shouted.

"Andrew – guess what?" he began. "I'm the killer and you took my ultimate goal away from he. You took my main agenda away from me! You killed Mother!"

Andrew didn't know what to do, here he was reuniting with his big brother and now finding out his brother was the Clydebank Ripper, and all the while feeling sick and disillusioned. Foam and blood dropped onto the floor in front of him, as his big brother stood in front of him holding a knife. Then he felt it, the blade dig deep into his stomach, he could feel the blade tear through his stomach wall. He could feel the stomach acid rise into his blood stream. He knew he was going to die tonight, he knew he was dying.

Zach stabbed and stabbed into his brother's body, watching him jerk and shield himself with every cut made. Andrew turned and began staggering along the hallway making his way

216

to the bathroom. (A safe room perhaps?) He got in, but his stalker followed close behind. Andrew turned to face his brother and was pushed into the bathtub. He cracked his head on the ceramic tub and lay there, blinking through blood-shot eyes as his attacker was above him bringing the knife down again and again and again.

For whatever reason the voice shouted, "Zach turn the bath water on, fill up the bath and drown the little bastard!"

He followed the orders precisely, just like a soldier would follow in the army.

The water began covering Andrew and was turning into a nice pool of blood. Andrew screamed and screamed, but all that came out was gurgling noises. The water covered his head, and within minutes Andrew became another victim of the Clydebank Ripper.

He watched as his little brother fell away into the darkness; he saw the once true light die in front of him. He turned to walk out the bathroom and back to the living room when a male voice spoke, "You ought to drink the bath water that got to be fun!" He turned back and lifted a cup off the sink and delved his hand into the dark blood water that surrounded his little brother. He brought the cup up to his lips and took a long swig of it. He smiled.

"Well done son, well done indeed," the female voice told him. "He will never take your identity away from you. Now go get your dad!"

He smiled.

48
Officer Down in Victoria Park
20th August 2000

It was a hot summer's day and the park in Partick was crowded. However it wasn't men and woman, boys and girls, young and old that crowded the park having picnics and walking hand in hand and doing fun activities. The place was crowded with police.

The Partick police division was on site after receiving a call from the morning park attendant.

Detective David Fellowes was called to look at the crime scene. Detective Fellowes was young and highly respected in the police force for his intellect and helpfulness in and around the Partick area.

Detective Fellowes was based only in the Partick division but had many ties with the surrounding police divisions – that being Drumchapel, Maryhill, Clydebank and Knightswood.

Detective Fellowes entered the fossil centre and on entering was met with a police officer throwing up his breakfast into the bushes next to the door, and a further two officers standing at the main entrance covering their mouths and noses with a handkerchief. Fellowes made his way into the crime scene and was confronted with the horrific remains of what was once a police officer, what was once a human being. He found the forensic examiner and walked over to him. "So what we got Sid?"

The examiner stood up. "Well David, it's a man, a policeman. Skinned and well hung up to drain of blood. He's a police officer, some of your guys found his squad car down outside the gates and his ID confirmed it was him."

David nodded his head. "Anything else?"

Sid looked at him. "Yes one more thing. Come with me."

The Detective followed the examiner who in return showed him the writing:

DO YOU SEE THE LIGHT OFFICER WILLIAM LIGHT?

"Do you know what that means David?" Sid asked.

David nodded. "Yeah, that's aimed at that officer from Clydebank – William Light, you know the officer whose son Andrew is wanted in connection with the killings in Clydebank and with the murder of his mother Sandra Light?"

Sid nodded after remembering. "So I would say by the looks of it, Officer William Light is the main target in all of this. How do you want me to process this now then?"

"Just do the normal Sid," David responded. "I'll contact the

Chief in Clydebank, inform them what we have here and hopefully he will do the rest from his side."

"Do you think it's the ripper again?" Sid asked.

David nodded. "Well, all we know about the ripper case is that each murder was different from the previous one and each one since the first one is far more brutal. This one seems to be far worse than the other ones though."

"Well I've seen my fair share of dead bodies, but this takes the gold medal for being the worst. I'll process the scene and get the report on your desk as soon as."

The detective nodded and walked back outside. He turned to one of the police officers manning the entrance, "Make sure the media and public stays away from here and make sure he's OK," he said, pointing to the officer who still was vomiting everywhere. The detective pulled out his mobile phone and dialled the Clydebank police station. It rang for a few seconds before being answered. "Hi can you put me through to Alex Grimm? Thanks. It's Detective David Fellowes from Partick police station."

He waited a few seconds, listening to the noise they called a song being played over the phone while he was on hold.

"Hello, Alex Grimm speaking," the voice down the line came.

"Hi Alex, it's David Fellowes from Partick police station here, we have a situation that has came up that literally has your name written all over it."

"Hi David," Alex began, "what's happened?"

David told him what had been discovered and told him about the writing that indicated that it was aimed at William Light.

"OK David," Alex replied. "I was actually wondering why there hadn't been any more killings for a while, I wondered if our main suspect had fled Clydebank and Summerston and changed his hunting ground to Patrick!? Leave it with me David and I'll send a few of my ripper squad down to you, to get details. I'll also inform William – got to get that guy 24/7 protection. I think his son is going to kill him!"

"So it's still Andrew we are all looking for then? A twelve year old boy is killing these people? Butchering them?" David asked.

"Unfortunately – yes," Alex answered. "The boy decapitated his own mother, so he is capable of anything. You have a copy of the picture we passed round of him?"

"Yeah got it," David replied. "Listen Alex mate, this is bad down here, real bad. You got to protect William fast, because if his son Andrew is doing this, who knows what he is capable of doing next!?" With that he hung up on Alex and made his way out of the park and to his car.

49
Time to Move
12th May 2000

He slept near to thirty hours after he murdered his brother. Slept in his bed, not wakening up once. Well that's what drugs do to you - heroin was his next fix and it knocked him out for what felt like forever.

He loved it. No more worries, no stress.

When he sat up, the smell was overpowering, the smell of death. Then the voices kicked in.

"Zach it's mother," the female voice said soothingly. "Zach, go check on your brother – the smell is so overpowering, I can't concentrate!"

He raised his hands to his head. "Not real, not real, not real!"

"Zach," came the voice again, "do as you're told!"

He gave in and got out of bed. He made his way along the hallway to the bathroom; opened the door slowly and walked in. The smell of death lingered in the air, he switched the light on and walked over to the bath and peered in.

Andrew lay there, still dead. Still wet, but now looked a nice shade of blue. (Cold water would do that.) The body was also full of goose-skin, or anserina cutis, which is roughening, or pimpling of the skin, he had skin maceration, or washer-woman's skin, which is swelling and wrinkling of the skin, the only thing that wasn't happening at this time was adipocere, which is the transformation of the fatty layer beneath the skin into a soap-like material – this process requires many weeks or months – Andrew now looked like a old man.

He stared at his dead brother, cocking his head to one side.

"What do I do now?" he asked himself. "This is my home and now I share it with a dead body. What do I do?"

It took a while, but an old man's voice started talking to him. "Zach, it can take weeks, even years, before the body fully decomposes. You can relocate, move away, and make a fresh start."

"I can't just now," he shot back, "I've got too much to do. Maybe in a few months time I'll move."

"OK Zach," a female's voice spoke next, "if you can handle the smell then that's OK with us. But we urge you to look for a new location now, so once it's time to move on, you will already have a place called home."

He nodded. "OK." He stepped out of the bathroom, turning the light off, putting his brother's body in darkness again. He reminded himself if he needed to wash or bathe at all he would just go to the local swimming baths, pay for swimming but take a shower instead. He smiled, but knew a new location would be ideal – somewhere no one can see from the streets. Somewhere hidden from view. Somewhere in the middle of nowhere. Some place like a forest. Then it came to him; his dad was born and raised in the Drumchapel – a small town between Clydebank and Bearsden. His dad told him about the woods that looked over Drumchapel and stretched right back to Faifley and Milngavie. Woods where a few times terrible things happened, things that made headlines in the papers: like the rape of girls and murders of innocent people. His father once told him of a girl who was raped and then hung from a tree by members of her own family. These woods also had a bit of superstition surrounding them; a circle of trees on top of the hill at the back of the woods was nicknamed the witches' circle. A place where supposedly witches chanted and preformed sacrifices.

These woods were called the Bluebell Woods, but soon he would call them home.

50
A Town Zach Now Calls Home
10th June 2000

There are many interesting things to see in Drumchapel, he read in depth on Google. He was so engrossed in it; it felt like he travelled back in time, to when Drumchapel was first built.

He printed off an in depth map of a trail and headed off to the starting position on the so called map. He was hoping to find a new home, off the beaten track so to speak. The starting position was Drumchapel train station.

Drumchapel – a town founded in 1858, and was going to be his home from now on. He got off the train and began walking towards the path to his new home, he walked down the stairs and turned left onto Garcadden Road and proceeded under the railway bridge. He passed by an old school on his left used as a workshop for adults with learning difficulties. He decided to turn round and head up to Old Drumchapel Road, he turned right passing an old petrol station on his right and bypassed a hospital perched on a hill. He walked for a further twenty minutes before turning left onto Kinfauns Drive and crossing over and onto the grass. He followed a pathway which winded in and out of trees and bushes before forking into two paths, one back onto Kinfauns Drive and the other into the Bluebell woods. His new home.

Drumchapel was going to feel the pain and suffering which ate at him inside.

51
Break-Up of the Relationship
30th August 2000

"This is getting out of hand William!" Nancy screamed at her man. "Your son, your youngest son, is wanted for murdering all those people and to think he turned up here and your daughter answered the door to him! She could have been next!"

William paced back and forth from the window to the living room door. "What do you want me to say or do Nancy? I've been kicked off the case!"

"Say or do?" Nancy said through gritted teeth. "Say or do? Your son knows where you stay, where WE stay! He is out there, hiding and waiting to strike again. Your boy Andrew killed all those people, including his mum! For crying out loud, he killed his MUM!" Nancy sat down, trembling, with tears flowing down her face.

William turned and walked over to her. He crouched down next to her and held her hand, but she pulled her hand away. "Nancy, honey, Andrew is the presumed suspect, just because he murdered Sandra doesn't mean he killed all those other people in Clydebank!"

"Just because," Nancy began, "just BECAUSE he murdered his mother? Are you seeing through black tinted glasses? For Christ's sake William you are a cop, you met up with your son, your son told you he killed his mother, your ex-wife. You and the police force found her headless body. Didn't you?"

William nodded and stood back up. He paced to the window. "We are searching for him. What more do you want me to do?" William said through gritted teeth. He spun round and looked at her.

Nancy shook her head. "I think it's best if myself and our daughter leave here and go somewhere safe. Maybe to my mum's in Edinburgh."

William went pale. "What? You are just going to leave me?"

Nancy stood up. "Honey it's the best way, while Andrew is out there and until he is caught it is best that we just end it. I don't want our daughter to come to any harm."

Tears rolled down both their faces but it was William who rushed over to his fiancée. "Please Nancy, don't do this not to me, not now!"

Nancy wiped away her tears. "It's the best thing, just until he is caught." She moved away from him and went into their bedroom, followed closely by William, still pleading not to go.

Nancy packed up most of her clothes and accessories, and did the same for their daughter.

Within a half hour, she was sitting in the car, daughter alongside her in the passenger seat strapped in, clutching her Barney teddy bear. William leaned in for a kiss but Nancy turned her head. "Let's just leave it there honey, phone me as soon as he is caught. I love you William but this is for the best." She rolled up the window, started the engine and drove away into the distance, and out of William's life.

William stood on the pavement as he watched his family this time walk out on him.

52
The Discovery of Andrew Light
2nd September 2000

Left decomposing in a bathtub for long enough left Andrew Light as just bones with his skin melting off into thick masses which floated in and around him.

A smell engulfed the close, almost like a rotten egg smell. Andrew's body had broken down and didn't resembling a human being anymore. Water continued to run and poured over the sides of the bathtub, dark blood red water flooded the bathroom floor, pouring into the floor.

Andrew Light was no more. Andrew Light became another victim.

"Yes hello, can I have someone out? I seem to be getting flooded from the upstairs neighbour. Yes, it's like rust coloured water coming through my ceiling. Yes, yes I've tried banging on the door, but to be perfectly honest with you; I don't think anyone has stayed there since May this year. Yes I'm sure its water, just a deep orange colour; it's like a tea stained colour. Yes, my name is Jeff Brown, I stay at 15 Alexander Street, Clydebank, and yes it's the Blue Triangle homeless unit. I'm ground floor and the rust coloured water is coming through my bathroom ceiling. Oh I meant to say there is an awful smell as well, like a dead rat or something. Yes I know the floors are concrete and nothing can get trapped between them, but there has been a vile smell all through summer. Yes I did call yourselves and your inept repairs inspector came out and done nothing apart from tell me to open up my windows and let some air in! OK, so when will the plumber come out? Good, good and remember and tell him that there is no answer to the neighbour upstairs, so he'll possibly have to break open the door. Yes I know you'll need the police for that but I don't want my house ruined. Please just do something today before my whole house is flooded." Jeff hung the phone up and waited for the arrival of the West Dunbartonshire Council repairs team.

TWO HOURS LATER

Jeff stared out of the living room window and watched as the councils repairs team drove up to outside the tenement block of flats. They pulled in and Jeff noticed that they did indeed call the police.

Jeff rushed out of his front door and met the repairs team and police officers in the landing; he guided them into his house and showed them the bathroom.

On entering the police noticed the rotten egg smell. They left Jeff's house and made their way upstairs to flat 1/1 - the flat occupied by Zach Light.

The ginger-haired repair guy from the council knocked on the door and awaited a response. They knocked again and waited once more.

"Nah there's nobody answering, but we need in there!" the guy said to the officer.

The police officer nodded and took one swift kick at the door and burst the lock open. The police entered first and checked each room, starting in the living room. The place was a rubbish tip: bottles, cans, food takeaway cartons lay everywhere. Then they spotted blood, the elder of the officers turned to the council workers, "Stay there until we say it's safe." They nodded. Both officers carried on through the house, they checked the bedroom, the kitchen and lastly the bathroom where they found the problem.

Lying in the bathtub, liquefied to just a mass of ooze, lay the body of once a human being.

The smell was over-powering; the insects crawled and buzzed about the body. The maggots squirmed their way through the last of the meat that clung to the body's bones.

The officers brought up their breakfasts.

"Control this is Officer Reilly, requesting emergency services including coroner and forensics to be sent to flat 1/1, 15 Alexander street Clydebank, over."

The radios crackled and dispatched responded. The officer that made the call answered, "Dead body, possible homicide over and out."

Both officers left the house and told the repair team that no work would be carried out. They informed the neighbour that made the call, and although shocked he was able to tell them that the boy that lived there went by the name Zach Light.

Alarm bells started ringing in the officers' heads - Zach Light – now where had they heard the name Light from before?

53
The Media Gets Another Slice of Action
2nd September 2000

DAILY RECORD
Bath of Blood
by Riley Hashcroft

Another body has been found in the small town of Clydebank that sits outside Glasgow.

This time a body, which is yet to be identified, was found in a flat in the homeless shelter called the Blue Triangle.

Police were called along with the repairs team of West Dunbartonshire Council, due to a neighbour complaining of being flooded from the neighbour above and of a foul smell coming through the ceiling.

WDC repairs teams couldn't gain access to the flat, so police were called in and on entering they discovered a grim find.

The badly decomposed body was found in a bathtub with the water still on and flowing over the side.

Police have yet to identify the body; however neighbours claim that the person staying in the flat was a young man that went by the name of Zach Light. However they are not ruling out that the body is not that of Mr Light.

Strathclyde police have issued a statement asking Mr Light he please contact Strathclyde police on 0141-555-7252.

Police are speculating that the most recently discovered body is yet another victim of the so-called 'Clydebank Ripper' - who has claimed five victims ranging from old to young. The first victim was discovered on January 19th.

The coroner based at the Western Infirmary has stated, "that due to the body being so badly decomposed, it looks as though date of death was sometime in May."

Police are looking for any witnesses to come forward if they have any information in regards to this latest victim.

Police are also looking at a disappearance of a young female called Lucy Windum, who was last seen in Pitmally Drive in Drumchapel, police also ask for witnesses to come forward for this case, but are ruling out anything to do with the Clydebank murders.

54
Dancing in the Moonlight
23rd September 2000

Spoilt for choice with both Indian and American Bar Grill cuisine, the Sunset Boulevard Hotel was the place to be on a Thursday -well known as 'Grab-a-granny' night. Friday, Saturday and Sunday were for the over eighteens only. The Boulevard had its own downstairs bar called Belushi's Bar and Diner, and also was home to the award winning Bombay Grill restaurant, two nightclubs and modern, yet comfortable, accommodation. The hotel is literally central to almost anywhere. Loch Lomond in Balloch, was only a twenty minute drive and Glasgow City Centre was at least thirty minutes away.

The nightclub itself opens its doors at 10:30 p.m. and is on till the wee hours of the morning. It was a fusion of test tubes and spirits when it was born in 1992 and christened The Sunset Nightclub, and together with Belushi Bar and the Bombay Grill they are one quarter of the Dormitory of Decadence that is Boulevard Hotel.

The locals call it the Boule.

He called it the slaughterhouse.

The voices told him to go out in a big way; prove to the public, to the world, that they were dealing with a psycho. That his aim in his sordid life was to kill his parents - but his brother spoiled that for him by killing their mother. However, his carcass is now lying on a coroners table while the good old police and forensics went over who exactly is that body found in his old house.

The media was flapping their wings over this huge story. Is this Zach Light, son of police officer William Light? Has he been murdered by his crazy young brother Andrew Light? What was the message all about with the skinned police officer found in the fossil grove in Victoria Park?

He knew he didn't commit the murder in the park. He knew it was his once good friend Jacob Kane trying to show the fine police officers that it was him, but surprise surprise, the police didn't know shit. They couldn't put two and two together, so that was left on the back burner. They thought his wee brother was the killer stalking the streets of Clydebank and above all else, although there were murders after Andrew died in May, Andrew was still chief suspect as he was 'missing'. He smiled as he was patted down by the security officers at the door of the nightclub.

The big well built guy nodded. "Right on you go." He walked past, went to the window and paid to get in.

"Let the slaughter begin at midnight son," the voice resounded in his head. He nodded and made his way to the bar. He didn't sweat as much as he thought he would.

The first floor was busy already: R&B and rap was favoured on this level, and anything from 2pac to Eminem was played constantly here.

He looked around; there were a lot of pretty girls, and a lot of the usual sluts looking to get laid by anyone or anything.

Girls wearing very short skirts, some wearing hot-pants - yes it was September but that didn't stop these girls from flaunting their bodies!)

He smirked and looked at his watch - 11:23 p.m. - not long now. He decided to go up to the next floor and see how busy it was up there.

He climbed the stairs, hearing the bass thumping and volume turned way up loud and the floor shaking underneath him, as though he was in an earthquake.

He entered the next floor, lights and strobe lights flashing in sync to the terrible rave music, music he didn't like or enjoy - and by the looks of it, nor did anyone else! He counted at least a dozen, maybe fifteen, people on the dance floor and at the bar, so he decided that it was the R&B floor that was to be the slaughterhouse.

He walked back down the stairs and looked out to the entrance: he counted three bouncers searching people for drugs, weapons and even chewing gum! (No chewing gum in the club as it sticks to the floor and is hard to clean – apparently.)

He walked back into the first floor; he looked about at the fire exits: one just past the toilets on the left and one just right of the bar. He studied the CCTV suspended from the walls and ceilings, and knew that he would be recorded when he carried out his plan.

He looked back at his watch - 11:55 p.m., five minutes to total impact, so time to go to the toilet.

He made his way to the toilet and passed by a few drunken guys as they stood at the urinals, he entered the second cubicle and locked the door. He placed his left foot on the toilet seat and removed his boot, he pulled out the insole and there lying underneath was his weapon of mass murder – four Stanley blades.

He removed them and fetched some sellotape - he had a small roll stuck inside the leather tongue of his boot. He began cutting strips of the tape and stuck the blades to the fingers of his left hand. He flexed his hand in and out, testing the blades and then took a sheet of toilet paper and raised his hand and slashed through it, the paper tore in half - good test, but that's only paper - it was time to try the real thing.

He pulled up his black hood and un-clicked the door latch. He left the toilet and entered the dance floor again, the place was busy and he thought he blended in just fine.

He looked at his watch - midnight. The voice sounded in his head like a starter pistol at the Olympics, "Time to be famous Zach!"

Another song came on; the words of the song rang oh so true through his head, he smiled and smirked at the lyrics from a rapper called Eminem, the song that was blaring from the speakers was "Criminal".

He smiled and was about to move onto the dance floor, when he was approached by a well built bouncer: skinned head and what looked like muscles on muscles.

"Hood down mate!" the bouncer said sternly to him. He cocked his head to the left and ignored him. "I said hood down mate!" the muscle bound wannabe wrestler said again. Yet again he cocked his head, this time to the right. The bouncer was getting angrier, he obviously wasn't getting his way this time. That's when the big guy stepped into his safe space; he raised his razor blade left hand and swiped the bouncer directly down his face. The bouncer, although shocked, stepped back raising his hands to his face as four long cuts poured blood.

"Help!" the bouncer screamed. But the calls for help were short lived as he stabbed the bouncer repeatedly in the stomach area. The bouncer fell to the ground.

People started screaming as he slashed and swiped his way through the dancing terrified crowd. Blood splashed onto walls, into drinks, onto other clubbers; people fell onto the dance floor and got trampled in the chaos. Bones cracked under the weight of people trying to flee the bloodbath, trying to remain alive.

He slashed his way through a crowd, a nineteen year old girl: smoking hot, wearing a boob tube and a very short white skirt, stared him in the eyes as he grabbed her by the hair and stuck the blades into her throat, in and out, faster and faster - the way she thought she was going to have sex tonight – hard and fast. The blood spurted out through the severed artery. She collapsed in a heap – dead.

He continued his path of destruction and then was met by a wall of bouncers: big and heavy, muscles upon muscles. He stood there amongst the sea of blood red, amongst the bodies that he had carved up. He flexed his left razor hand, a bit like Freddy Kruger would in *A Nightmare on Elm Street*. He nodded as the bouncers rushed him, one by one, and one by one they fell at the feet of him - stabbed in the throat, in the chest, the stomach and also the eyes.

Carnage was the scene and carnage was his task. People ran out into the cold air away from the madman, as he walked through the bloodied dance floor. As he was just about to leave he heard whimpering from behind the bar, he stopped and turned and walked over to the bar. He peered round and saw a young barmaid cowering, shielding herself from the horrifying attack. He cocked his head and walked over to her. He grabbed her by the hair, she screamed but he didn't listen as he marched her over to the CCTV camera and stood in front of it, the barmaid pleaded, cried and wet herself as he looked up at the camera. (With his hood on, the camera could only pick up the darkness that surrounded his face.) He raised the razor hand and slashed the terrified barmaid across the throat, he pulled back her head and let the blood spurt out and down her uniform, and then he tossed her to one side like a rag-doll.

He heard sirens in the distance, the police were coming, it was time to act fast, do what he had to do and leave via the fire exit and run and hide in the fields outback.

He went back over to the bar, found a marker pen and among the dead bodies on the dance floor he began to write:

REAP WHAT YOU SOW.

He smiled and walked at a steady pace out of the fire exit door and away into the night just before the armed response unit of Strathclyde police entered the premises.

He moved through the thick grass and weeds and watched as the police combed the area.

The end game was now in sight.

55
And the Results Are?
10th September 2000

The police officers all gathered in the meeting room of Clydebank police station. They all were waiting for the Chief to give them details on the body found in the bathtub.

Was it another victim of the so called 'Clydebank Ripper'?

Alex Grimm stood in front of his officers. 'Guys, can I have your attention please?' The room became silent as the officers all listened to their boss. "The police forensics report is back on the body in the bathtub, and it turns out due to decomposition, the only way to identify the body was by dental records. The body is that of our prime suspect Andrew Light."

The entire room started whispering between themselves.

"Now calm down guys please," Alex told the room. The room became silent again. "Yes, this does mean that our prime suspect is dead, but surprise, surprise - now we have to figure out who killed him."

Moans and groans escaped the officers in the room.

"But Chief," an officer at the back standing against the wall with his arms folded began. "Do we have to really investigate his death? I mean the son of a bitch is dead and gone, it's over!"

Whispers again engulfed the room between the officers - chants of 'yeah the bastard is dead' and' thank God for that!'

"It's our duty to fulfil the investigation of the death of someone," Alex explained to the room. "Now as it stands, we have cordoned off the house that Andrew was found in, and starting today we will question neighbours and surrounding buildings if they have seen anything strange. Maybe whoever killed Andrew is just scared of what he or she has done. Maybe they are hiding. I have found out from West Dunbartonshire Council that the house where Andrew was found is part of a homeless section and that the person registered as staying there was none other than Andrews's brother, Zach."

Whispers began again throughout the room.

"Quiet please," Alex shouted above them. "Yes Zach Light is, or should I say was, staying there. He is now listed as missing as he's not been seen for months. What I believe is that Andrew went to Zach and confessed all about the murders and the abuse suffered at the hands of his mother and Zach thought he would stop it in its tracks by killing the murderer.

Yes, maybe he has done us a good deed but we now have to hunt for him. I will get CCTV to go over all footage with regards to the blue triangle homeless section. Now I need you guys to get out there and start looking for him. This is an old photo we found in his mother's house of him, pass the copies between you all and bring the guy in. Please remember if you do come across him, he may be scared for what he has done to his young brother. Just inform him that all will be OK."

The officers all nodded and took a copy of the photo of Zach; they got up and left the briefing room.

Just as Alex was about to leave the room, he was shouted on by the desk sergeant. "Chief, phone for you."

Alex nodded and followed the desk sergeant. He picked up the phone, "Hello?"

"Hi Chief, you are looking for the wrong person," the voice on the other end said.

"Who is this?" responded Alex.

"You found Andrew's body I see!" the voice replied, "and now you are looking for his brother Zach – the killer of the ripper. Well Chief, I've got news for you. Zach didn't kill Andrew, and Andrew wasn't the Clydebank Ripper. The person you are looking for is talking to you just now. I hope you are good at puzzles Chief, anagrams to be precise because you will have to solve this puzzle in order to know who I am. My name is Jake Bacon. Ha ha ha. Oh alright Chief, here is a wee clue for you: I love my wife and I love bowling."

The line went dead. "Hello?" Alex said. "Hello?" He slammed the phone receiver down. 'Fucking God damn it! Sergeant get that call analyzed and get someone to crack this fucking puzzle, this, this anagram – JAKE BACON. The killer is not Zach Light. Also get in touch with William Light, tell him his life might be in danger and make sure the rest of the guys find Zach, he may be in danger.

He hung the phone up in the telephone box outside the 10 O'Clock Shop on Garscadden Road and smiled.

Now it was time to put his old friend well and truly in the frame for all the murders. Yes he knew Jacob Kane had killed his wife, her lover and her lover's son. Yes he knew that he skinned that police officer and left him dead in fossil grove in Victoria Park and blamed him for it.

Now the game was coming full circle, and soon both he and Kane would meet to finish off what had begun as a great friendship.

It was time to put Kane all across the papers, all across the television. It was time to bring Kane out of hiding to kill him once and for all.

56
The Depression of William Light
23rd September 2000

The feeling of depression is deeper, longer and more unpleasant than the short periods of unhappiness we all have from time to time.

This presents a very bleak picture. However, it's important to remember that depression isn't an absolute - it's not simply a case of either you're depressed or you're not. There's a progression from feeling blue to the full clinical illness described above. Even then, you won't suffer from every symptom.

Sometimes there may be an obvious reason for becoming depressed, sometimes not. There is usually more than one cause and different people have different reasons.

It may seem obvious why – there may be life events or changes in circumstance such as a relationship breakdown, bereavement or even the birth of a child – but sometimes it's not clear. Either way, it can become so bad that you need help.

Often people don't realise how depressed they are, because the depression has come on gradually. They may try to struggle on and cope by keeping busy. This can make them even more stressed and exhausted. This can cause physical pains, such as constant headaches, or sleeplessness.

Depression is also a feature of many other illnesses and conditions, which may need to be checked for with tests and investigations. These 'organic' causes include:

An under-active or over-active thyroid gland

Vitamin B12 deficiency

Viral infections

Stroke

Parkinson's Disease

Traumatic brain injury (head injury)

Dementia

Chronic inflammatory conditions

Cushing's Syndrome

Chronic painful disease such as osteoarthritis

The symptoms of depression include:

Losing interest in life

Finding it harder to make decisions

Not coping with things that used to be manageable

Exhaustion

Feeling restless and agitated

Loss of appetite and weight

Difficulties getting to sleep

There are however two types of treatment available: talking treatments and medication. Both can be accessed through your family doctor.

Talking treatments consist of:

Counselling helps you to talk about your feelings in private with a sympathetic professional. Your GP may have a counsellor at the surgery.

Cognitive behavioural therapy can help to overcome the powerful negative thoughts that are part of depression.

Interpersonal and dynamic therapies can help if you have difficulties getting on with other people. A relationship counsellor might be helpful if you're having difficulties with your partner.

If you have a disability or are caring for a relative, a self-help group may give you support.

Medication side consists of:

Antidepressants can be effective if depression is severe or goes on for a long time. They may help feelings of anxiety and help you to deal with problems effectively again. The effects of antidepressants won't usually be felt straight away - people often don't notice any improvement in their mood for two or three weeks.

As well as tablets, an alternative remedy called St John's wort is available from chemists. There is evidence that it's effective in mild to moderate depression. It seems to work in much the same way as some antidepressants, but some people find it has fewer side effects. You should discuss taking it with your doctor, particularly if you're taking other medication.

Like all medicines, antidepressants have some side effects, although these are usually mild and tend to wear off as the treatment goes on. The newer antidepressants (called selective serotonin reuptake inhibitors) may cause nausea and anxiety for a short while. The older antidepressants can cause dry mouth and constipation. Unless the side effects are very bad, your doctor will usually advise you to continue taking them.

Four out of five people with depression will get better without help. The shorter the time you have been depressed, the better the chance that it will lift on its own. However, even with treatment, one in five people will still be depressed two years later.

There is support:

It may be enough to talk things over with a relative or friend. If this doesn't help, talk it over with your family doctor.

Talk to someone close to you about how you feel. Going over a painful experience and crying it out can help you come to terms with it.

Get some regular exercise. This will help you keep fit and sleep better. Do jobs around the house to take your mind off thoughts that make you depressed.

Eat well, even if you don't feel like it. Don't drink alcohol, as this makes depression worse, although it might not seem to at first.

If you can't sleep, try not to worry about it. Do something relaxing in bed such as reading, watching TV or listening to the radio.

If you know what is making you depressed, write it down and think of ways to tackle it. Pick the best ones and see if they help.

Keep hopeful - this is a very common experience and you will come through it, probably stronger and more able to cope than before.

Helping someone who is depressed consists of:
Listen to them but try not to judge them. Don't offer advice

unless they ask for it. If you can see the problem behind the depression, you can help the person to find a solution.

Spend time with them, listen to their problems and encourage them to keep going with activities in their routine.

If they're getting worse, encourage them to visit their doctor and get help.

William Light threw the pamphlet down on the rubbish engulfed living room carpet: papers, leaflets, discarded pizza take-away boxes and just plain old rubbish.

The place had become a rubbish dumpsite since Nancy left him with his baby girl in tow.

He knew it had become dangerous, but not knowing if they were alright was getting to him, to that extent he knew he was falling into depression.

One son had murdered his ex-wife and then according to the newspaper, this son nicknamed 'the Clydebank Ripper' has been murdered himself. His other son was reportedly missing and to top it all off, he was suspended from the police force as he got 'too involved' with the cases.

Now William sat in his empty, stinking house, drinking enough beer to embarrass even the worst alcoholic. William Light had become depressed and just wanted to die.

He sat on his crap infested sofa, watching crap on the television and drinking cheap crap beer (Asda smart price lager - 4x100ml cans for £1.00). He hadn't shaved or washed since Nancy left him, his normal black stubble on his face had now become a hide-away for lost pieces of food.

William sat there twiddling the sharp kitchen knife in his hands, rolling it back and forward. He knew he was depressed, that's why the doctor gave him the leaflet, but the leaflet didn't say anything about your son being a killer now did it!?

He always wondered about how simple it would be just to either slash his wrists and watch his life disappear in front of him or just plunge the knife deep into his stomach and bleed to death.

He read somewhere that a stab wound to the belly, if it involves the abdominal aorta or inferior vena cava, would lead you to bleed to death fairly quickly, within a minute or two. A wound to the smaller vessels will take longer to kill you. However if you avoid all major vessels then death will take days to weeks from infection if no medical attention is received. On the other-hand, he contemplated slitting his wrists, but he had also read somewhere that it depends on how you cut them. Cutting straight across the wrist horizontally would be ineffective. When people cut their wrists, they are severing (or attempting to sever) their radial artery, which is a fairly large artery. If it is cut straight across and all the way through, the artery will constrict and draw back into the wound and very effectively stop the bleeding fairly quickly.

If the artery is cut vertically, the body's own defence (the artery constricting) will actually pull the cut open and cause it to bleed more profusely. It showed an example that if you take a piece of hose, and make a small slit down the middle, then pull from each side of the hose, the cut opens up - same concept.

Death from exsanguinations (bleeding out) from your radial arteries would not be very quick. First heart rate goes up; you become pale, clammy, lethargic, dizzy, and light-headed. Then you start to become short of breath, like starving for air and you can't get a full breath, eventually your blood pressure starts to drop until you loose consciousness. Finally, you will have lost so much blood that there's not enough left in your cardiovascular system to circulate to your organs and you die. This process could take hours, or minutes. The wrists, could take up to an hour or more.

The knife, the sharp knife fell from one hand to the other. William ran his thumb across the blade, the blade cut his thumb and a small droplet of blood came out of the slit.

William sighed. "The wrists it is then!" He rolled up his dirty sleeve and balanced the knife long-ways on his right wrist. "Here goes. Nancy please forgive me, God I'm sorry!"

As William was about to swipe the blade across his naked wrist, a loud bang came from the front door. He jumped and dropped the knife. "Fuck!" he screamed. He got to his drunken feet and swayed a bit before steadying himself and walking to the front door. William peered through the peephole and saw his boss, Alex Grimm, and another police officer standing with him.

"Fuck, fuck, fuck!" he mouthed under his breath.

"Come on William open up, we know you're in there!" came Alex's voice from through the door.

William looked back at his disgrace of a house and muttered again under his breath, "fuck, fuck, fuck!" He reluctantly opened the front door.

When the door opened fully, Alex and the other officer stepped back because the stench was overpowering.

"Jesus Christ William," Alex began, "what the fuck are you doing?" The chief barged passed him, followed closely by the other officer.

"Well why don't you just come right in Boss!" William replied sarcastically. He closed the front door over with a bang and staggered into the rubbish tip that once was a living room.

Alex stood in silence looking at the mess: the rubbish, the beer and wine bottles. "Seriously mate, what the hell is happening to you?"

William walked over to the coffee table and picked up an opened can of beer. He took a swig from it and then offered it to his boss and the officer. They both just stared at him.

"You get your fucking act together, you hear me?" Alex shouted at his best friend.

"Why?" William began. "Why should I? My missus left me with my kid, I got suspended from my job, BY my boss should I add! My youngest son killed – sorry butchered - my ex-wife, killed a lot of locals and then turns up dead himself. So tell me boss – why should I get my act together? Eh? Tell me, come on!"

"William," Alex shouted walking over to him and smashing the can of cheap lager out of his hand. "Andrew is not the killer and Zach is missing. We got a call telling us who the killer is, but we are trying to decipher the anagram of his name!"

"What?" William looked confused. "What the fuck are you saying? What anagram?"

"It's two words and the killer said a clue," Alex told him.

William staggered over to the fireplace and picked up a piece of paper and a pen. He walked back over to his boss. "What's the anagram?"

Alex looked confused. "Why? Do you think you can solve it?"

"I fucking love puzzles and *Countdown*'s conundrum is my highlight of the day. So tell me it." William started to look, and feel, sober.

Alex removed a piece of paper from his suit pocket and unfolded it. "JAKE BACON," he told his friend. "At first we checked Google and typed in Jake Bacon but nothing came up."

William wrote it down and started moving letters about.

Five minutes later, his eyes went wide and he looked up at his boss. "I know who it is!"

"Who?" Alex asked.

"I interviewed the bastard at the beginning of the year, February I think, we brought him in on suspicion of murdering his wife, her lover and a little boy. The bastard supposedly committed suicide by jumping off the Erskine Bridge." William looked enraged.

"Who the fuck is it?" Alex asked again.

"His name is Jacob – Jacob fucking Kane!" William said.

Alex pulled out his radio and informed the police station.

The hunt was now on.

57
Number One Suspect – Jacob Kane
25th September 2000

THE DAILY RECORD
IS THE NET CLOSING IN ON THE RIPPER?
Reported by Mark Wilson

Yesterday Strathclyde police revealed the name of the suspect still at large for the murders in Patrick, and most importantly in the district of Clydebank. Jacob Kane, a family man from the Bowling area of West Dunbartonshire, is wanted in connection with various murders that took place through out this year. DCI Alex Grimm had this to say - "Strathclyde police are looking for one suspect in the murders that have taking place during this year. Andrew Light, who was found murdered himself, was the main suspect up until his name was cleared due to a phone call I received from a man we believe to be the actual killer. At first we were looking for Andrew Light, and then in relation to his death, his older brother Zach Light. But after receiving a cryptic clue as to who the killer was, we enlisted the help of both Zach, and Andrew's father William Light, who helped us crack the cryptic clue and made us aware that it was the suspect we now seek - Jacob Kane."

As reported months ago, via the Clydebank Post, Jacob Kane was presumed dead as well after his wife was murdered. He had apparently jumped from the Erskine Bridge that crosses the River Clyde and connects Renfrew to Old Kilpatrick - his body was never recovered. At the time Jacob Kane was the main suspect in the murder of his entire family, except for his young daughter. He had allegedly murdered his wife, her lover and a four year old boy in his house in Bowling. After being questioned, he disappeared and then the murders started happening in and around the Clydebank area.

Andrew Light was seeking his father, who had moved back to where he was born in Drumchapel, only to tell his long lost father of the grisly murder he had committed. Andrew Light informed his father, who in turn informed the police station, that Andrew had killed his mother. Police raced to William Light's old house in Summerston and discovered the remains buried in the back garden of his ex-wife Sandra Light.

Months later, more murders happened, and Andrew Light was now missing. A few months passed and Andrew Light's body was found in the homeless unit in Clydebank, in a house belonging to his elder brother Zach Light, who in turn was now missing and presumed to be the killer of his brother, the

Clydebank Ripper. Zach Light is presumed missing at this time. After police received Andrew Light's autopsy results and the phone call from Jacob Kane, we now advise the public of Glasgow to take extra care at night and if you see Jacob Kane to stay well clear of him, as he maybe armed but is extremely dangerous.

The victims of Jacob Kane's murder spree are as listed below. All have now been laid to rest.

- *Mrs Julia Robertson (72)*
- *Miss Hayley Williams (21)*
- *Mrs Sally Kane (28)*
- *Mr Edward Simpson (32)*
- *Mr Edward Simpson Jnr (4)*
- *Miss Danielle Winchester (16)*
- *Mr Colin Jefferies (57)*
- *Mrs Ruth Kane (69)*
- *PC Brian McKay (34)*
- *Miss Monica Thompson (19)*
- *Mr Andrew Light (12)*
- *Mr Nick Bennett (39)*
- *Sunset Boulevard massacre: 6 in total – names withheld*

Detectives now turn their case to looking for Zach Light, the missing eldest son of PC William Light.

Police have been told by psychologists that it is 'highly likely' that Jacob Kane always had the urge to kill and that the catalyst for his spree was the discovery of his wife's affair.

The families of two of Kane's alleged victims last night called for the return of the death penalty.

*

Kane sat on the park bench just west of Byers Road, rage engulfed him as he read the headlines. His name was getting throwing about like trash. Yes he had killed his wife, her lover and the guy's kid. Yes he had killed and skinned a police officer, and yes he had killed his mother, which has never been reported. But Kane knew he wasn't the Clydebank Ripper. Kane knew he didn't kill this Andrew Light, or indeed abduct his older brother Zach Light. Kane knew that it was Zach who was the Clydebank Ripper, and Kane knew it was time to finally put their so called friendship to sleep once and for all. It was time to finally face Zach and end this battle. Kane knew he wasn't going to clear his name, he knew he would be up for manslaughter. Kane knew one more body getting added to his tally wouldn't really change the fact that he was heading to prison for a long time.

Kane folded up the newspaper and left it sitting on the park bench, he was in the lovely woodlands that ran from the Glasgow Botanical Gardens literally the full length of Great Western road and surrounding areas, the woodlands overlooked the River Kelvin which joined onto the River Clyde at some point down the road.

Kane walked at a slow pace down the pathway, walking with his gloved hands in his pocket, his white fur lined jacket zipped right up his chin and his hood up. Winter had finally landed in the city of Glasgow, dubbed the home of, 'four seasons in one day'.

His blood boiled and the anger was building up in the pit of his stomach, he knew there was only one way to really end this, and that was to kill Zach Light, but at the same time all he cared about was his young daughter - who he had left in the safe haven of the derelict house they had both slept in.

Kane bypassed a young boy, around sixteen years old. The young man nodded and smiled, "Alright big man."

Kane didn't respond. Then came the next phrase from the young man, "Hey big man, I said alright, least you could do was acknowledge me!"

Kane stopped and turned and faced the young guy, he cocked his head to one side and then pulled down his hood.

The boy's eyes went wide with fright. "Yo...you're...that guy the police want, you're...you're Kane, Jacob Kane!" he stammered and stuttered and tried walking backwards, only to trip and fall on the wood barked covered pathway. Kane took a step closer, and closer, and closer once more until he was standing tall over the young, frightened man. Kane pulled his gloved hands out from his pockets and bent down to the terrified boy; he put his hands around the neck and pulled him up to his feet. The boy was that frightened he urinated in his jeans. Kane looked down and then looked the boy dead in the eye.

"Please Sir, don't hurt me," the young terrified lamb said. "I'll do anything!"

Kane cocked his head. "Anything?"

"Anything!" the boy pleaded.

Kane half cocked a smile on his face. "I need you to send a message to Strathclyde police, tell them the game has just begun!"

The boy's life ebbed away from him with one quick crack and twist of his neck.

Kane felt the vertebrae crack below his fingertips as another young life disintegrated in front of him. After the life ended Kane carried the dead weight over to the iron railings that were the public's protection from the raging water. He propped the young dead man up against the fence, looked around for any other signs of human life - seeing none, took out a piece of paper and wrote the words:

3 KILLERS

2 BROTHERS

1 REVENGE

After leaving his mark, he stuffed the paper inside the mouth of the boy and pushed the dead body over the railings and watched as it fell down into the River Kelvin - another body to add to his tally.

Kane smiled and thought to himself, *two can play that game!* He pulled up his hood and headed back to see his daughter.

58
Two Can Play That Game
26th September 2000

EVENING TIMES
Late Edition
RIVER HORROR AS BODY IS FOUND
Reported by Peter Burgens

A POLICE probe was launched today after a body was found in the River Kelvin in Glasgow's West End. The grim discovery was made by a passer-by who spotted the body in the river, near the Kelvinbridge, at around 0715 hours. Emergency services raced to Great Western Road, with police, ambulances and fire crews on the scene, early this morning. Police said it is not known how the person got there, or how long the body was in the water. Officers sealed off a large section of the river bank, around Great Western Bridge, and scoured the river's banks. Witnesses said there were around a dozen police cars and ambulances at the scene, and more than twenty emergency services staff. Paramedics from the Scottish Ambulance Service's elite Risk and Resilience unit also attended. A recovery operation, involving police divers and a rescue boat from Strathclyde Fire and Rescue, was carried out. The body was removed from the water around an hour later. A large section of the busy road was cordoned off and police stood guard at the scene, just yards from Kelvinbridge Subway station. Meanwhile, forensic officers combed surrounding streets and nearby parkland for clues. A spokeswoman for Strathclyde Police said, "We received a call around 0715 hours today of a report of a body in the River Kelvin. The incident is currently ongoing. Emergency services are at the scene to recover the body."

A post mortem is due to be carried out to establish the exact circumstances surrounding the death. Commuters faced rush-hour delays as police cordoned off a large stretch of Great Western Road to carry out investigations. Drivers heading towards Glasgow city centre were caught up in queues of more than two miles, with traffic backed beyond Anniesland Cross.

*

Kane sat next to his daughter reading the paper and smiled.

Zach read the newspaper and knew what was happening.

Strathclyde police were stumped.

William Light was scared.

271

59
A Grimm End to a Friend
28th September 2000

He watched from a distance away, knowing too well if he was spotted, he would have to answer questions:

What have you been up to?

Where have you been?

Why did you kill your brother?

Do you know Jacob Kane?

He watched the chief of police stand at the entrance of his father's house, he watched his dear father - who looked a shadow of his former self - getting words of encouragement from his best friend.

Grimm was his name, Chief Inspector Alex Grimm to be precise, and he was the one who received the call from 'Jake Bacon', but it turned out that his dear old daddy is good at anagrams and figured out, much to his delight, that the ripper was none other than Jacob Kane.

He smiled, he had set Kane up and now Kane was getting angry, in fact that angry, Kane had already taking out his anger on another poor defenceless boy.

But all in all, he liked this. His main aim was to kill his mother, but sadly she had died at the hands of his younger brother Andrew. His next aim was to kill his father, and the net was closing in on him. He had relocated to Drumchapel to get closer to his father and watched him from a distance away. He had found out that his girlfriend had left him, with a young girl in tow. (His daughter perhaps!?)

Now he stood at least one hundred feet from the house that his father stayed in, he stood and watched as his father and his father's best friend talked about the case in hand.

He smiled.

"Time to put a grim end to his friend son!" the woman's voice told him from within his head.

He nodded.

"Time to show him, that you are the killer, that it is you with the pure hatred in your cold eyes!" said the man in his brain.

"Kill the Grimm Zach, kill him now!" the woman cackled.

Zach pulled up his black hooded top and put his hands in the pockets of it. He played around with the blade, stroking it with his thumb.

He watched as Grimm bid his friend a farewell and walked down the stairs. The inspector got into his car and started it up, he put the car into gear and drove off down Southdeen Avenue and left onto Kinfauns Drive, on his way back to the police station.

Just before Grimm got to the lights at the junction of Old Drumchapel Road and Kinfauns Drive he sprinted across the grass and walked round the side of the car to the driver's side. Grimm pulled up to the red light and waited for the lights to turn green, that's when he struck.

He tapped the window and Grimm jumped with surprise. Grimm looked at the hooded figure and then rolled down his window.

"Can I help you?" Grimm asked.

He just cocked his head to the side.

"Are you OK son?" Grimm asked.

Just then he raised his left fist and punched Grimm directly in the face, instantly knocking the Chief Inspector out. Grimm flopped forward onto the steering wheel, and Zach looked around, people walking up towards the traffic lights, stopped and watched at what was unfolding in front of their eyes. People pointed and whispered. But no one interfered.

He opened the door and pushed Grimm over into the passenger seat and then climbed in himself. The lights had turned to green and he drove away, not right but left up to Bearsden Road.

"Take him to the park Zach, the park!" the voices screamed with excitement.

"What park?" he asked, putting his foot on the accelerator.

"Mugdock Country Park: the best place to display another work of art, to send a message to everyone!" the voices replied.

He nodded, smiled and continued to drive up Bearsden Road towards Mugdock Country Park.

Mugdock Country Park is a country park and historical site located partly in East Dunbartonshire and partly in Stirling, in the former county of Stirlingshire, Scotland. It is to the north of Glasgow, next to Milngavie.

The park includes the remains of the 14th-century Mugdock Castle, stronghold of the Grahams of Montrose, and the ruins of the 19th century Craigend Castle, a Gothic Revival mansion. The park has a moot hill and gallowhill, historical reminders of the baronial feudal right, held by lairds, of 'pit and gallows'. Natural features include the Allander Water, Mugdock Loch, and Drumclog Muir. Visitor facilities include a visitor centre and cafe in the former Craigend Castle stable block, and a garden centre in the walled garden.

He pulled up just outside the park, darkness was setting in, and he got out and walked round to the passenger side. He opened the door and pulled the unconscious man out; he pulled him up to a walking position and literally dragged the man deep into the park and off the beaten path.

Down near Mugdock Loch, he let the body of the Chief drop to the ground.

The man moaned, starting to fully come awake again. The bruise on his face was turning a nice shade of purple. He looked down at Grimm and cocked his head to one side.

Grimm fluttered his eyes open and tried to concentrate on the blurry image standing tall above him.

"Jacob Kane?" he managed to mutter.

He just stood there, cocking his head from one side to the other. Then he shook his head from side to side.

"Who are you then?" Grimm asked trying to sit up and then get to his feet, but he was forced back down by a heavy boot on his chest.

He raised both of his hands, pulled the hood down and stared at his intended victim.

"It's you!" Grimm stuttered. "Zach...Zach Light!'

Zach smiled.

"Why you doing this?" Grimm questioned.

"To see what your insides look like!" he answered.

Grimm's eyes went wide with fright as he pulled out the

knife and plunged it deep into Grimm's stomach.

The defenceless man screamed in agony as he twisted the blade deep inside the stomach, and then pulled the blade up towards his chest area. He pulled the knife out and every time Grimm breathed hard, the wound opened wide and blood poured out. He watched as Grimm's intestines tried to force their way out of the body with an urgency to escape.

Grimm clawed at his stomach, trying to hold his internal organs in, but with no such luck.

Within minutes he had claimed another victim on his quest for revenge against his father.

He breathed hard and long as he watched the Chief Inspector's life ebb away into the darkness.

He made sure no one was looking and then pushed the body behind a bush in the mean time so he could go and retrieve the dead man's car.

Ten minutes later he was back with the car; he pulled alongside where the body was hiding and opened the passenger door. He picked up the dead body and placed it into the passenger seat. Closing the door, he got in himself and drove away back down towards Drumchapel.

The dark had finally settled in for the night as he pulled up outside his father's house. The streets were empty, which made it even more fantastic for him, as he pulled the body out of the car and onto the spare ground in front of the houses on the street. He propped up Grimm's body against the white rusty goal posts that stood on the ground and with a piece of rope tied the body to the post.

He stood back and admired his work. Then producing a piece of paper he scribbled the words:

I AM THE RESURRECTION AND THE LIGHT

He went back to the dead man's car, started up the engine and drove it onto the field. As he neared the body, he revved up, floored the accelerator and drove the car directly at the Chief Inspector's limp carcass. As he neared it, he jumped out and watched as the car smashed directly into the body.

A fine mess for Strathclyde's finest to find.

He pulled up his hood and headed back over to his father's house. As he neared the street, an explosion from behind him lit the dark sky up above Drumchapel.

That's when people started noticing something was wrong on the field.

Police, ambulance and fire crew were called as he climbed the outside stairs of the tenement that his father stayed in.

He watched people looking out their windows at the scene he had caused. Just his luck - the close door was open. He walked in and turned left to his father's house. He raised a hand, he knew that what he had caused outside would create a distraction from what he was about to do. He knew that if the police and emergency crews were dealing with what was left of the chief inspector and the car, then he could literally get away with killing his father once and for all.

While the close was engulfed with the bright flames from the burning car, he raised a hand and was about to chap the door when the door creaked open. He cocked his head, looking puzzled he entered the house anyway pulling out his knife at the same time.

He closed the door behind him and studied the hallway first – it was in total darkness. He walked up a bit and stared into the kitchen – all was silent and dark. He turned and began to walk into the living room, where the lights were also out, but the darkness was flashing bright orange flames with red and blue lights flashing in sequence.

Puzzled, he was about to turn and go up the hallway to one of the bedrooms when he heard it, it was faint but he heard it.

A mumble or a moan of some kind. He turned and studied the living room area again. He looked at the black felt chair that stood to his right and saw – nothing. He looked to his left, stood in front of him was another black felt couch, this time a two-seater. He saw nothing on the couch again. He was about to leave when he heard the soft mumble of a moan once again. He decided it was definitely coming from his left, possibly behind the two-seater.

Clutching the knife in his left hand, he walked around the back of the couch only to see a figure tied up in the midst of the flashing blue and red lights and orange flames– his father.

William was bound at the ankles and wrists with duct tape. He had a piece over his mouth, which explained where the mumbled moans were coming from.

He smiled.

"Easy prey," said the woman's voice in his head.

He nodded. Then the blackness engulfed him as he took a blow to his head.

60
The Showdown
29th/30th September 2000

He fluttered his eyes open, adjusting to the darkness once again. His head hurt like a son of a bitch.

Where was he?

All he remembered was killing the Chief of police and then going to finally kill his father.

And then darkness.

He looked around and saw hunched body of a woman in the corner.

The world around him was filled with pain. His head was the world and it hurt bad, real bad.

"Please, don't hurt me!" The woman's cries were strangled from fear but still shrill, piercing the gloom of the night. Unfortunately for her, she was currently tied with duct tape at both her hands and feet. There would be no help for her.

He blinked once trying to see where he was and who she was and then he saw him, his best friend turned enemy, Jacob Kane. Kane didn't even bother gagging her as he slammed her against the wall by her neck, reducing her cries to gasps for air. The sadist in him called for her pain, pain on a level equal to his constant suffering. He was filled with nothing but an uncontrollable desire to make her bleed.

Kane raked his eyes over her, but felt no stirring of desire. If he was to rape her, it would purely be to make her experience the shame of being helpless and violated. There was no point in it all. What he needed was her hurt. What Kane saw in front of him was purely a toy before he killed Zach.

Kane pulled out a knife with his other hand he stabbed her heart and dragged it sideways, opening up her torso in a gush of blood that splattered over his clothes. The woman's cries sharpened for a moment, before fading out along with the light in her eyes.

Jacob let the body slump to the ground, as he gripped the knife fiercely. The adrenaline was still rushing through him, and the sounds of his own heart were pounding in his ears.

Lifting the knife, he gave it a long lick, tasting the sharp metallic taste of the blood. It was intoxicating. The blood drove him even higher, sending his mind into a blissful ecstasy.

It was the only time he could escape from the pain that plagued him, the torment of the past that refused to go away.

The blood was just like her lies. He was hooked onto it, just as he had been in the past. With them he had escaped from reality and experienced happiness in a world of his own. There was no truth in that world, but there was no pain either.

His hands trembling from the high, he accidentally cut his tongue. It barely affected him. If anything, it heightened the buzz in his mind.

Convulsing uncontrollably, Jacob stood up and breathed heavily then looked towards his main aim – Zach. He towered over the dead girl, compulsively swallowing his own blood. It was choking him but he didn't care.

In his world, there was no pain.

Kane watched as Zach moved his head, allowing the blood to trickle down his neck from the small wound on the back of his head. He tried to move but couldn't, his hands and feet were bound to a chair, which he knew he was sitting in.

He was a prisoner. But out of the darkness came a voice, this time not in his head. He tried to loosen the restraints but couldn't and then the voice showed himself.

"Hi Zach, remember me?" Kane smirked, stepping out of the darkness and into the view of him. He cocked his head to one side and looked at his one time friend, the person who had saved him from killing himself, his partner in the crimes he had committed against other humans.

He cocked his head to one side and growled.

"Now Zach, is that any way to treat a friend?" Kane teased. "Oh that's right I'm not your friend anymore. I'm the guy you are trying to frame for YOUR murders!"

He tried his hardest to escape the restraints but to no avail. He just stared at his captor.

"Oh wait you'll love this!" Kane made him jump with surprise as he backed back into the darkness. "What's behind door number one Zach?"

Kane opened the door and pulled, with brute strength, something large but immobilised, bound and restrained just like his once best friend.

He stared at the other hostage – it was his dad, it was William Light.

Kane threw the police officer to his side just in front of him, he tried again to escape his restraints and yet again to no avail.

"Now Zach," Kane began, "it's not worth trying to escape, you are stuck here with me and we are going to end this." Kane moved over to where William lay bound and gagged, picking up a chair and moved back to where Zach sat. "Do you know where you are Zach?"

He looked around from the chair he was strapped into – all he saw was darkness and moonlight from outside.

"So do you know Zach?" Kane asked again, he leaned forward and glared at Zach in the eyes.

He shook his head.

"This place is rich in history, a story to tell your children's children, a place that has survived the Clydebank blitz, when the Germans were bombing the UK. This is a place where you and your father will die. But for now…"

Kane stood up and picking up a steel pole raised it high and swung it at Zach's face. Blood poured from another gash above Zach's eye as he went limp.

Blackness engulfed him once again.

The Titan Crane in Clydebank is a 150-foot-high (46 m) cantilever crane that was built in 1907. It was designed to be used in the lifting of heavy equipment, such as engines and boilers, during the fitting-out of battleships and ocean liners at the John Brown & Company shipyard, then the biggest shipbuilding group in the world. The category A Listed historical structure is earmarked for refurbishment by 2007 and will become a tourist attraction and museum about shipbuilding in Clydebank.

A £24,600 order for the crane was placed with a Dalmarnock based engineering company, Sir William Arrol & Co. in 1905. Titan was completed two years later. Originally it was designed for 160 tons lift capacity, however this was upgraded to 200 tons on the turn of the Second World War when it became apparent that the original specification would be insufficient to lift new long range gun barrels onto ships.

Now he awoke once again, engulfed with darkness but hearing muffled moaning coming from close-by. He blinked once and then again, adjusting to the darkness. It was total darkness outside and inside. He tried moving again, but he was still tied to the chair. He looked to his left and saw his father propped up at the wall of the building. His father looked at him with pleading eyes: eyes that needed help, eyes that were scared, terrified even.

"So Zach welcome to the Titan Crane here in Clydebank," came Kane's voice from the shadows. "A historic category A listed building – granted it's been through the wars – no pun intended there! And now it is your grave, where you go to sleep forever, and well your father there, you know that piece of shit propped up over there? The one YOU were going to kill. The one that started all the rage inside you, brought the darkness out of your soul and showed the real world pure evil, well he's just…well a bonus so to say! But not yours; no, no, no he's mine. You want to blame me for your killing spree, well I may as well just take some bodies." Kane stepped forward holding a black handled chef's knife, it glistened in the moonlight, and Kane smiled. "Tonight you dine in Hell!"

He pulled and tugged at his restraints, and one hand finally became free just as Kane came closer to him. He managed to free his other hand and legs just as Kane swung the knife at him. He dived out the way, onto to the debris that mixed with the pigeon feathers and faeces, just as Kane brought the knife down on the chair. He quickly got up from the floor and turned to face Kane, he breathed fast and hard, his shoulders heaving up and down as both him and his enemy stared eye to eye.

"Ah so it's a fight you want Zach?" Kane glared.

He cocked his head and smiled at him then he heard her. "Zach it's your mother – time to kill this guy. Cut him up, make HIM go to sleep!"

He smiled and picking up a steel pole he stomped across the floor towards Kane, who now grasped tightly the knife in his right hand. As he swung the pole at Kane, Kane swung the knife catching him on the arm, leaving a thin trail of blood flowing from a small cut. The pole caught Kane on the shoulder knocking him back a few feet. He moved in for the attack on Kane while his nemesis was dazed and swung the pole once again, connecting with Kane's left leg, he heard the crack as steel met bone. Kane fell to the ground in agony as he advanced once more standing over him. Kane looked up at him and he looked down at the now pleading man in front of him. He cocked his head to one side before finally giving Kane the knock out blow.

Kane fell into darkness, the tables had turned.

61
I Spy
30th September2000

William watched as his eldest son tied Jacob Kane up. The rope that was used on his son was now used on Kane. William shuffled and moaned where he was seated.

After he had finished tying Kane up, he turned to his father and knelt down in front of him. He removed the duct tape from over his father's mouth.

William inhaled some air and looked up at his eldest son, after a few minutes he muttered the words, "Zach, you don't have to do this. I'll get you some help – I promise."

"Don't listen to him Zach," came the voice, "he caused this. He left you with me, left you with me so I could abuse you."

He cocked his head to one side and looked into his father's terrified eyes. He stood up and took a deep breath, his shoulders heaved up and down. His mind was conflicted . One part wanted to end his father's life. (That was his sole purpose in the first place!) Hell, he has been handed his father on a silver platter anyway! And then the other part was telling him to let him go, that he has suffered enough. Before he had made up his mind, his captive started to moan. He spun round, looked at Kane and smiled.

"Please Zach, don't do anything stupid," came his father's voice.

He spun round and glared at his father. "Stupid? Don't do anything stupid! Let me remind you Dad, you and the bitch of a mother caused this. Stupid doesn't even come into it!" He marched back over to his father, bent down and cut him free from the restraints. "Leave, go now and don't worry, I'll get you soon, I'll get you my way. Nothing changes – you will die, I will kill you!"

William stood up, pale as a ghost and backed towards the exit of the crane. "Please forgive me son."

"Go NOW!" he screamed at his father.

William turned on his heels and sprinted towards the stairs.

Zach walked towards Kane. "Waken up friend."

Kane stirred in the chair before blinking his eyes open and starring at him.

"Kane – I want to play a game."

Kane looked puzzled. "Just kill me, you fucking prick!"

Zach smirked. "All in good time my friend." He undid the restraints on Kane. "Make any funny moves and I'll gut you here and now, and you won't see your little girl anymore."

Kane gave off a shocked look on his face. "You leave her out of this."

"Aw, what's the matter Jacob? Did I hit a nerve?" he grinned as he grabbed him by the collar and dragged him outside onto the viewing area of the crane.

"I always knew you were a pansy Zach, you need my hands tied because you know I would skin you alive. I'm warning you, you prick, touch my daughter, lay a hand on my daughter and I'll kill you, do you understand?"

He laughed. "That's going to be hard especially when you're..." he cut short as he pushed Kane over the railing.

Kane closed his eyes awaiting the impact of the hard surface below him, and then opened his eyes. He was upside down looking at the skyline of Clydebank, looking at the old shipyard buildings of John Brown's engineering company.

Kane looked up and saw he was dangling from a rope tied around his legs, and then he saw him.

Zach stood peering over the railing at Kane. "I-Spy Kane!"

"What?" Kane growled. "Fucking let me up, come on let me go!"

"I said I wanted to play a game, so I spy with my little eye something beginning with G?" he smirked.

Kane swung backwards and forwards. "Fucking let me up

you fucker!"

"Can you not guess it?" he shouted down to him.

"Fucking let me go – NOW!" Kane screamed.

"OK, OK," he began, "it's ground, it's right down there about a hundred feet below you, you can't miss it!" With that he let the rope go and watched as his one time friend - a man he saved from suicide, a man that helped him kill, a man that became his enemy - plummet to the muddy ground below him.

Kane screamed all the way down and landed hard amongst the debris and mud that once was a great shipyard.

Zach peered over the side of the railing for a few minutes more, just to make sure Kane was dead before looking to the left and seeing his father standing at the bottom of the crane.

William looked on in horror as Kane fell to his death; his oldest son had just killed another man. He stood awestruck, gob-smacked and utterly speechless as he didn't know if Jacob was telling the truth.

Was Zach behind all the murders?

Was Zach the Clydebank Ripper?

William stared at the body of Kane – a mere hundred feet away from him, and then he stared up at his son, standing tall at the top of the crane.

The victor?

He looked down at his father and cocked his head to one side, and then he was away from the railing - heading down the stairs to the ground to finally kill his dad.

62
Daughter Now Cared For
27th September 2000

"Now baby," Kane said to his daughter while stroking her soft hair, "remember Daddy loves you very much. But we can't stay here any longer, and Daddy has some unfinished business to take care of, so the people in this house will look after you, and Daddy will be back soon OK?"

It was late at night and Kane had placed his daughter, curled up in a blanket fast asleep, on the steps of a newly built house in the West End of Glasgow.

"This house belongs to my great Uncle Charles and great Auntie Edwina," Kane continued, "they will look after you from now on. You can't be with Daddy anymore sweetheart, it's too dangerous. But I promise to God that I'll be back for you." He bent down and kissed his daughter on the forehead, and producing a piece of paper he wrote down:

Great Uncle Charles, this is my daughter Rebecca. She is two years old and was born on the 21st of December 1998. Please can you raise her, the way you began to raise me before my *mother came back into my life. Uncle Charles, I as you may now know, am a serious wanted man and a serial killer. I have killed and helped kill a lot of people in and around the Glasgow area. Including: my mother, my wife, her lover and her lover's son. I am a sick and evil man but was once a really good guy. I think my wife caused me to be this way. As you might also be aware it was reported in various newspapers that I committed suicide by jumping from the Erskine Bridge – that, Uncle, was a lie, made up by myself and my friend at the time - Zach Light. My friend Zach saved me that day so to speak with reasons I thought were for the best, but it turned out he wanted me to help him in his revenge against his mother and father. Charles, I won't go into details but all I can say is yes I did help him, but not in killing his mother and father. We both killed a lot of people, that I for one am not proud of. Charles please keep my daughter safe as this will be the last time I see her, I have unfinished business to take care of and won't be back until it is done. You can take this as a confession if you so wish to do, just please watch after my daughter and raise her the good way.*

Uncle Charles thanks.

Jacob

Kane folded the note up and tucked it inside the blanket with his young daughter, giving her a kiss on the forehead once more. He wiped the tears from his eyes and rang the bell on the door before high-tailing out of sight away from the front door.

Crouching low in the bushes Kane watched as the door of the house opened, and there standing on the doorstep peering out was his great uncle Charles, he looked left then right and then down and that's when he saw the two year old girl, he bent down and saw the note poking out of the blanket, he opened it and read it. Kane watched as his uncle raised his hand to his mouth in shock, and then he picked young Rebecca up and carried her inside. The door closed behind him.

Rebecca was now safe.

63
Whatever Happened to Nancy?
30th August 2000

Nancy and her daughter waved goodbye to William as they made their way out of Drumchapel and off to Edinburgh, to Nancy's mother's house. Nancy wiped away the salty tears as they fell from her eyes. She kept checking her daughter who sat in the car seat in the back of the car via the rear-view mirror. She then concentrated on driving; she headed right onto the main road of Drumchapel, Kinfauns Drive, and then right onto Drumchapel Road before hitting Great Western Road just off of Blairdardie Road. After about fifteen minutes she left the ramp and merged with the M8 and continued onto the Glasgow/Edinburgh Road. Her mum stayed in Harthill, which literally sat slap bang in the middle of Glasgow and Edinburgh - 32 Hirst Road was her mother's address. She continued onto the M8, and before long she turned left into Hirst Road and parked her car outside her mother's house.

Her mother was there to greet both of them on the driveway, where cuddles and more tears were shed. Her mother ushered her into the house and sat her down.

"I've been following the news honey. Is it all true? Is it William's youngest son who is doing the murders?" said the well kept, middle aged woman.

Nancy nodded. "Yeah, just don't say much in front of missy over there, you know what she's like. But yeah, Andrew is his name, apparently he – you know..." she lent forward and whispered, "killed his mum and buried her in the back garden before carrying out the Clydebank murders. I had enough mum; I mean after he turned up at our door and then met up with William and told him what he had done – that was the last straw. So I told him until it is safe, me and the little one will stay here. I hope you don't mind?"

"Mind?" replied her mother. "Of course I don't mind, after your father passed last year I could do with the company, and what better company to have than my daughter and grand-daughter!" she smiled that old woman heartfelt smile, that made Nancy smile back.

"Thanks Mum, for everything." Nancy said before standing up and giving her mother a cuddle.

Just as Nancy let go, the house phone went. Her mother went over to it. "01501-555-2244. Uh-huh, yip, two wee seconds and I'll get her for you." Nancy's mother turned round. "Nancy, it's William."

Nancy got up and went over to the phone, taking the receiver off of her mother.

"I'll make another spot of tea," her mother said before shuffling off to the kitchen.

Nancy nodded before raising the receiver to her ear. "Hi William, are you OK?"

A laugh came from the other end of the line then came the words, "You wish it was William!"

Nancy's eyes went wide with fright. "Who…who is this?"

"Let's just say I'm the guy who is going to kill your fiancé, and then I'm coming for you!" came the reply then followed laughter.

"Andrew is this you?" Nancy asked bravely.

No answer came as the line went dead.

"Hello? Andrew? Are you there? Is anyone there?" Nancy quivered.

Her mother came rushing through to the living room again. "Is everything OK sweetheart?"

Nancy shook her head. "No Mum, I think that was Andrew. I think he's done something to William, I have to phone him." She got another dialling tone and dialled her house; the phone rang and rang before eventually being picked up.

"Hello? Hello William? Honey is that you?" Nancy said in a

high pitched voice.

The other end crackled. "Yeah it's me babe, what's up?"

Nancy breathed a sigh of relief. "I just got a call from what I think was Andrew!"

It went silent on the other end.

"William?" she asked.

"What did he say?" came the response from William.

"He said – you wish it was William and then he said 'I'm the guy that's going to kill your fiancé then I'm coming for you'!" Nancy blurted out fast.

"OK…OK honey, Nancy listen to me - phone the local police tell them the story, tell them who you are and where you are, ask them to come out and keep an eye on the house. Please baby, do it for me. If it was Andrew then we know that he is capable of doing something worse. Do not call me understand? Keep the line free, I'll call you morning, noon and night and check up on all of you - understand?" William spoke.

Nancy nodded then replied, "Yes."

"Stay safe babe – I love you." With that the phone went dead.

Nancy hung up and tears started streaming from her eyes, she shook all over and went white as a ghost. Her mother guided her over to the couch and sat her down, she then sat down beside her, comforting her.

"It's OK honey, listen John next door is a police officer, I'll get him and he can advise us what to do." She stroked her daughter's hair before leaving the room.

The phone rang again; Nancy peered over at the table on which the telephone stood. A moment of silence then it rang again. She stood up: scared, shaky and fearful of what was on the other end.

"Hello?" she said into the receiver.

"Hello Nancy," came the voice, "it's me Alex Grimm. Are you alright?"

Nancy gulped down the saliva which formed in her mouth. "Yes, yeah I'm fine Alex, thanks for calling."

"Nancy," Alex began, "William is just off the phone. He told me everything, just sit tight, don't leave, we will catch Andrew and stop him before he does anymore bad things."

Nancy nodded. "Uh-huh." She replaced the handset and sat back down.

Nancy knew deep down this was just the beginning.

William knew he had to protect his family, even if it meant stopping his young son.

Alex Grimm had called a meeting and was now surrounded by news media and angry public.

He stood in the phone box, laughing and smiling. He had managed to get Nancy's mother's phone number from direct enquiries, as she was listed in the phone book, he knew her name as Andrew told him Nancy's surname.

The game was now in motion, the hunt was on for Andrew, and he knew he could continue his quest to kill his father as the police looked for Andrew, or what was left of him.

64
The Vision
30th September 2000

He dreamed the perfect dream, some would say a nightmare, but to him a perfect dream. His dream was how he was going to kill his father. He was dreaming now, he was wide awake but was thinking about the dream and how he had finally caught his father and took out the revenge that was ideal to the man that left them with the thing they called Mother.

His dream was him slicing through the last strands of flesh. His father's head went rolling. He smiled as his blood splashed his cheek.

Warm blood felt so good on his cold skin.

He looked around.

Everyone that he wanted dead was now dead.

He envisioned himself as this mighty serial killer, an unstoppable force that would wreck havoc in Glasgow and could never die. He saw the headlines:

ZACH LIGHT – THE NEW FACE OF TERROR

He saw movies getting made about him, books flying off the shelves by world renowned doctors.

He saw his name in lights.

The lights of a killer.

He knew he wasn't going to be disappointed at the lack of fear in the air. Fear meant he was happy.

Apart from cutting off his father's head, he envisioned skinning him alive, just like what Kane done to the copper, but then again that was copying another killer and he was no copycat!

He let his knife cut into his father's skin and blood began to flow. He then pulled every organ out of his father's body, letting it fall to the floor.

He smiled, he was now the winner.

His task was done.

65
The Chase
30th September 2000

He got to the bottom of the Titan crane. He looked left saw the mangled body of his nemesis Kane lying amongst the mud, water and rocks.

He smiled.

Then he was off across to the old boat shed, where he saw his dear old dad head to.

"You got to kill him Zach," came the all too familiar voice. "Catch him, kill him!"

He nodded. "Don't worry, I will!" he started sprinting towards the old boat shed. He got to the tattered old door and forced it open using the pole he grasped in his left hand. He got in and scanned the place, he heard rustling coming from the back of the shed, and began walking slowly towards where the noise was coming from.

He stopped.

He cocked his head, trying to amplify the noise and then he heard it again, coming from behind some old rotten wood lying against the back wall, he made his way over to it raising the pole as he went, as he raised the pole, ready to swing at what he hoped was his father – out ran a large black rat, it scurried and squeaked away from him as rage overtook him and he turned towards the entrance to see his father squeeze out the entrance.

He made his way back out into the old dockyard and scanned the surrounding area: then he saw his dad running with all his strength to the old John Brown's shipyard administrating offices.

He smiled and swung the pole around in a 360 degree circle and began marching over to the run down building.

He smashed his way through the glass door and scanned the area once again, this time there was no sign of his father. He stood still and silent, listening for the slightest noise – a can falling, a rock dropping, a scuffle of a shoe. But there was nothing, until he felt the thump from behind him.

He fell to the ground and as he was doing so, turned onto his back, which was searing in pain. Standing above him, holding a fire extinguisher was his father, breathing hard and ready to swing the extinguisher once more. "Why are you trying to kill me son?"

He dusted off his jeans and began to stand up.

"Don't make any sudden moves son," William said. "I will

hit you again!"

For the first time in a long time, he now stood face to face with his father. The guy who left him with his abusive mother.

"Tell him Zach," came the voice from within, "tell him why you are trying to hurt him and then hurt him for real. Do it Zach, do it for us!"

He cocked his head. "You want to know why Dad?" he sneered. "You want to know why we have come to this point in time?" He backed up by two steps. "You see, you left me and Andrew – oh by the way yeah I killed him too! You left us with her, that bitch of a thing we called a mother, yeah Andrew told me what he did and when he told me, that's when I killed him. You see my plan was to make Glasgow notice that there was a killer on the loose and, while you and the rest of the pigs were searching for the killer, I would come after my dear mother and father. But that plan changed, Andrew killed my bitch of a mother, so I turned my attention to you, but I needed help. You see that sorry excuse for a man that lies out there in the mud, you know him as Jacob Kane? Well he thought I regarded him as a friend but what he didn't know is I watched him kill his wife, he sliced her throat up in the Kilpatrick hills above Bowling, placed her in the boot of his car and then dumped her with the rest of the bodies in his house: the bodies of her lover and his four year old boy. You let him escape. You, Dad, you caused him to join with me!"

"What the hell are you talking about?" William asked. He lowered the fire extinguisher to the floor, looking puzzled he asked again. "Explain to me what you mean?"

"One night, I watched as this sorry excuse for a man was about to jump from the Erskine Bridge, he was going to end it all, but I needed help to strike fear in the hearts of every Clydebank and Drumchapel resident in this area of Glasgow. So I talked him down, we staged his own death and he came and lived with me. It wasn't until late on in the summer where I decided it was time to use Kane in my game of revenge. Our first killing was that girl in her bed – hey did you and the cop pals like the note and kidney?"

William shook his head. "You sick son of a bitch, how could you do that?"

He smiled and then continued. "Well it was easy: I took a bat and battered her, and then I carved out her kidney, and sent it in the post – easy!"

"You sick son of a bitch!" William yelled. "She was just a kid!"

"Yeah Dad, and so were we when you left us!" he shouted back at his father.

"I...I asked you both to come with me," William replied. A tear formed in his eye.

"As I recall Dad, you asked Andrew, and him being the age that he was, wasn't exactly ideal, of course he was going to stay with Mum, but you didn't ask me Dad, did you? No you didn't, instead you left me, left us to be abused by her. I got out, but Andrew didn't come with me either, in fact he stayed there and got abused sexually by her. My mother, YOUR ex-wife, sexually abused your youngest child. Oh sorry, second oldest child now isn't it Dad? How are Nancy and your darling daughter anyway?" he snapped at his frail father.

"You better not have touched them!" William threatened.

"Touched them?" he said. "Dad, Dad, Dad - I fucking know where they are! She left you because Andrew turned up at your door and now she's in Edinburgh – well the outskirts of Edinburgh, anyway staying with her mummy. Oh I heard she got a crank call – now I wonder who that was from?" he said sarcastically.

"You God damn son of a bitch!" William yelled, rage and hatred building up inside of him. He clasped hold of the fire extinguisher once more and walked slowly towards his eldest son.

"Now, now Dad," he began, "don't want to do something

you'll regret." He grasped the pole tightly.

"Putting an end to you won't be something I would regret Zach!" William seethed with rage through his teeth.

As William raised the extinguisher above his head, ready to bring it down on his son, Zach swung the pole and caught his father right on the left kneecap. William dropped the extinguisher and fell to the ground. He stood above him and glared down at his fallen prey.

"Go do it," William said, wincing in pain. "Kill me you bastard, go do it before the police arrive!"

"Police?" he laughed. "You think the boys in blue are going to come and save you? Really?"

"They'll be here shortly, I made the call!" William replied, still nursing his wounded leg.

He looked puzzled and slightly lowered the pole. "How?"

William looked up at him and smiled. "Easy you dip-shit, on my phone!" William pulled the phone out of his trouser pocket.

Zach's eyes went wide. "No not like this, you have to die; it's all part of my plan!"

In the distance came the sirens, the cavalry were close by.

"Can you hear that Zach?" William began shuffling away from his oldest son. "That's the sound of you serving life in

Barlinnie you little shit!"

Zach lowered the pole, then smiled. "Problem is Daddy, you got to prove it first and then there's catching me. You see Jacob Kane is out there, he's your man, you only have what I told you stored in your brain and I don't think that's going to help you in a court of law!"

"Wrong again asshole!" William stated. "Try this on for size." William pressed a button on his phone.

What came out the phone was Zach's voice:

"You want to know why Dad? You want to know why we have come to this point in time. You see you left me and Andrew – oh by the way yeah I killed him too! You left us with her, that bitch of a thing we call a mother or should I say called, yeah Andrew told me what he did and when he told me, that's when I killed him. You see my plan was to make Glasgow notice that there was a killer on the loose and while you and the rest of the pigs searched for the killer, I would come after my dear mother and father. But that plan changed, Andrew killed my bitch of a mother, so I turned my attention to you, but I needed help. You see that sorry excuse for a man that lies out there in the mud, you know him as Jacob Kane? Well he thought I regarded him as a friend but what he didn't know is I watched him kill his wife, he sliced her throat up in

the Kilpatrick hills above Bowling, placed her in the boot of his car and then dumped her with the rest of the bodies in his house: the bodies of her lover and his four year old boy. You let him escape. You, Dad, you caused him to join with me!"

William turned the phone off. "Bye-bye son," he said sarcastically.

The sirens neared, and he saw out of the corner of his eye the blue flashing lights of at least four police cars. One in particular caught his eye – the armed response unit.

"Maybe I'll finish you off another day Daddy!" He ran at his father with the pole tightly grasped in his left hand, and as he neared his father, he swung and cracked his father's other knee. William screamed in agony and rolled over onto his front, only for Zach to pull out a knife and stab him in the back. More screaming came from William as he removed the knife, bent down and whispered. "Hopefully I've severed your spine, dear Dad, hopefully you'll never walk again! See you real soon Daddy!"

With that said, he ran out the door, looked to his left and saw the police car units. There were seven police cars: one riot van, two armed response units, one dog unit and three normal cars. He turned to his right and ran along the derelict ground of the once popular John Brown's Shipyard.

He vowed to himself, and to the voices in his head, that he would come back to finish off his father once and for all. He stopped for a breather and turned and watched as the police began searching the area, he smiled and looked down at his hand –- grasped tightly in his right hand was his father's mobile phone. He smiled and placed the phone in his pocket and headed into hiding…for now.

66
The Awakening
30th September 2000

The dogs barked and heavy boots thumped and squelched over the muddy ground. Clanging of metal against skin banged heavy in the night air.

"Can we get paramedics over here please!" the police officer said, kneeling down beside the mangled remains of the man known as Jacob Kane.

The crunching of boots again and the barking of the dog as the paramedics bent down next to the officer.

"Looks like he fell from up there!" the police officer told the paramedic, a middle aged man with thin greying hair.

"Oh hell, he's long gone." The paramedic said, nudging Kane's body.

"We'll pick him up later." The cop said, walking away as it began to rain.

The paramedics followed the cop as rain poured on Kane's body.

They paid no mind to the thunder or lightening.

"When we got the call from one of our own, we knew it was

going to be a long night; apparently there have been more murders!"

"Great, a whole night of rounding up bodies cause of some crazy son of a bitch," another cop said.

They headed inside the old boat shed to search for William with the rest of the police force.

Meanwhile, Kane was still on the ground. A lightning bolt struck the roof of the building as the investigators prepared to take Kane's body away.

"A few kids said they saw two guys fighting on top of the crane before Kane was thrown off and well landed on that." an officer said while pointing to Kane's body.

"Wrap him up, they'll do an autopsy...gee, I wonder how he died?" the paramedic joked.

"Yeah yeah," another paramedic said.

Suddenly, a bolt of lightning came crashing down, right on the crane; causing all three paramedics to fly backwards.

"JESUS CHRIST!!" one of them shouted, pulling himself up.

"You OK?"

"Yeah...I'm fine," he grunted, helping the other one up.

"Christ, looks like God really wants this guy dead."

"You're telling...holy shit...did he just move?"

"What?"

"His hand, it just twitched."

"No it didn't."

"Look!"

After a few seconds, one of the paramedics walked away.

"It moved, check his pulse."

The other paramedic walked back to the ambulance and reached for a pen.

Suddenly his mobile phone began to ring.

"Hello?" he said.

"Hey Dad," a familiar voice on the other line said.

"Hey son, what is it?"

"I was just wondering if you were coming home soon."

"Well we've got a big case here son, a bunch of bodies, I don't know if I can make it tonight, you need anything?"

"No, it's just dark out, and I was worried, since you do work with killers and all."

"Not killers son, killed," he corrected.

"Yeah well, just be careful, I don't want to lose you like I lost Mum."

"Don't worry son, I'll never leave you, I promise."

"I know," he said.

"Well do your homework and get to bed."

"Yes sir."

"And don't cheat off your friends; I don't want another call from your teachers."

"I'm sorry Dad; I was just under pressure, what with the test..." he began.

"I know, I know - life can be stressful, but you just have to work harder."

"Yes sir."

Suddenly a horrific scream and a nasty creaking noise could be heard from around the corner.

"Uhh, son, hold on."

"Why? What's wrong Dad? Dad? DAD?"

The paramedic slowly approached the scene; one of the other paramedics was laying on the ground, twitching.

"Steve?" he asked, slowly approaching him. "Steve?"

He rolled him over slowly...both his eyes were missing.

"OH MY GOD! What happened?"

"The...the...m...m...man...on...the...ground..." he chocked out slowly.

"The what?" he asked. Suddenly, he realized that Jacob Kane's body was gone.

"Dad, are you there, what's wrong?" the boy on the phone called, but his father was too preoccupied to answer him.

He stood up and backed up slowly, phone in hand.

He suddenly stopped when he backed into something.

He turned slowly, before he could even look, a hand violently wrapped around his face, two fingers digging into his eye socket.

He screamed and dropped the phone.

"DAD, DAD!" The boy shouted into the phone.

But no one responded, only screams.

"DAD, WHAT'S HAPPENING? DAD! Dad!" he said, unable to scream anymore.

Kane dropped the paramedic's body and watched as it thumped to the ground without its eyes, Kane raised a muddy boot and brought it crushing down on the paramedic's head. The paramedic's eyes were lying on the ground below Kane; Kane raised the muddy boot again and brought it down on the eyes making them burst their ooze all over the mud.

Kane noticed the phone lying near the dead paramedic's body; it lit up for its final time before Kane slammed a muddy boot on that as well.

"Dad...are you OK?" the boy began to ask, but the phone went dead.

"Time to get my revenge Zach. Time to kill you," Kane snarled before walking away into the dark night.

67
One Month Later
31st October 2000 - Halloween

It was a calm day, from the looks of things. Everything seemed so peaceful. The wind blew in the trees and he could see a teenage couple, walking hand in hand through the forest. The girl had light brown hair that extended down to her waist, peachy skin, and vibrant green eyes that rivalled the green on the trees. She wore a brown knitted sweater and black tights with grey trainers. The boy seemed to be at least five years older than her, standing a head and a half taller. He was wearing a dark blue sweater zipped up, faded jeans and trainers. He had jet black hair and snow white skin. His eyes were as black as midnight.

"Isn't it beautiful, babe?" the girl asked her boyfriend, Paul.

"Yeah, nice and peaceful too." Paul smiled sweetly, making her blush as she grinned. She giggled as she wrapped her arms around his neck and kissed him.

He watched as they kneeled down onto the carpet of brown leaves that lay below them.

"Do you want to?" the girl asked, smiling.

Go to Sleep

Paul gave a sly smile back. "Only if you are sure?"

He watched as she nodded, then began to undo her boyfriend's jeans. He watched as she took out his swollen member and began pleasuring him. The look on the boy's face was as though he had won the lottery.

He watched as he held her head against his crotch, cocking his head to the left and to the right. His urge to kill was getting to boiling point.

These were his woods. His home. These two highly sexed up teens were degrading his home.

It was time to move, time to end this little sex show and to reclaim his home back. He removed the hunting knife from the sheath attached to his belt and advanced towards the teens. He stopped when he heard the boy speak.

"What if I cum?"

She removed his erection from her mouth and smiled up at him. "So be it, I'll swallow just for you." She went back to pleasuring him.

He watched as the boy's knees buckled and he knew the boy was about to orgasm. That's when he made his move, he rushed forward and not giving the girl time to stand up, he raised the knife and swung it between her face and her boyfriend's body, severing the boy's penis in two halves. The girl fell back, choking on her boyfriend's severed penis and the boy fell back onto the grass, blood spurting out of his crotch. He screamed in agony and the girl cried as she spat the severed penis out.

He cocked his head to one side, before bringing the knife down onto the boy and repeatedly stabbing him over and over and over again. The girl couldn't move or say anything; she was frozen on the spot, watching as her boyfriend was being ripped apart.

Then as he watched the light go out in the boy's eyes, he turned his attention to the girl. He stalked her, slowly, and then picked her up and glared at her in her eyes.

"Pl…please don't, don't kill me." she stated, tears streaming down her face. "I won't tell."

The voice screamed at him in his head, "FINISH HER. FINISH HER NOW!!!!!"

He gave a sly smile, before running the knife over her throat and ripping open her skin. He stood back and watched as a fountain of blood poured from her neck, it looked like it was raining red.

Moments later she slumped to the floor of the woods – dead.

He admired what he had done and knew deep down that he would continue to do things like this, especially if anyone trespassed on his ground, the ground that is called the Bluebell Woods. He knew he had to stay hidden for now, but once all is clear and calm, it was time to start all over again.

He cleaned his knife, replaced it in the sheath and began concealing the bodies so no one would find them.

68
Two Months Later
21st November 2000

"You're doing great Mr Light."

"Cut the bullshit Doc," William said turning his wheelchair round to face his doctor. "If I was doing great I'd be walking, but unfortunately due to my spine being severed I ain't am I?"

"Mr Light," the doctor began, "your progress has came on good within two months, remember if your son had stabbed you just a millimetre to the left, then you would be dead. It was also lucky for the police to find you in time."

"Yeah, but can't say much about the bodies left behind though." William shook and then bowed his head. "I mean we have my son Zach, a frigging serial killer, still at large, we have Jacob Kane thought to be dead only to rise up and kill two paramedics and be on the run again; and then there's me - fucking confined to this contraption, not able to wipe my own arse, let alone even walk again. I swear I should have killed him while I had him down." William began crying.

"At least you have your fiancée and your daughter back. That's a good thing isn't it?" the doctor reassured.

"Yes and no, I'm stuck on benefits now for the rest of my life. We have to move as Zach knows where we stay, the press are never off our backs, oh and did I forget to tell you – I CANT FUCKING WALK!" Tears streamed down William's face.

"Listen Mr Light," the doctor began, "it's still early days. You might be able to walk again in the future."

William looked up at him. "Yeah and the good people of the United Kingdom will vote the Tories back into parliament!" He shook his head. "In case you weren't aware Doc – I was being sarcastic!" With that he turned and rolled out of the doctor's office, meeting him in the waiting room was Nancy and his daughter; his little angel rushed over and gave her daddy a big hug.

"All will be fine Daddy," she said, wrapping her arms around his neck. "You just wait and see."

69
The Future
5th January 2013

Dear diary,

I was thinking about him again. Not a boy, but a man; not a boyfriend, but my father. I can barely remember him; you see I was young at the time. He left me on the doorstep of my great uncle Charles, who without a doubt has raised me up well, shielded me away from the bad stories etc. But you see diary, I found out a lot about my father via Google, I just typed in 'Jacob Kane' and up popped 13,300,000 results with regards to that name. I had to scroll down until I found a news article in relation to my father, or as the press called him 'the skinner'. You see initially he was called 'the Clydebank ripper' but that title eventually went to another person. My father got the name 'the skinner' because he skinned a cop alive, for what reason I don't know, but according to the press it was to send out a message to the police and Glasgow.

I just never had the chance to ever meet my father. He is still out there in hiding, looking for the ripper, the police say its still an open case but to me it's thirteen years old, I'm fifteen now and haven't seen my dad since I was two. According to the papers and the letter left with me for my great uncle Charles, he says he was a bad man. But surely he's not now? I mean there have not been any killings, or missing people, reported in the areas that he once roamed about.

I remember reading an article entitled 'Local man survives 100 foot fall and gets up only to kill two paramedics'. My dad fell off the Titan crane and survived. Yet the man, the one they call 'the Clydebank Ripper' runs and hides. I found out his name was Zach Light, he murdered a bunch of people too along he is still out there. I know my father is hunting him, I know if my father finds him, he will kill him. But diary I'll say this only once, if my father doesn't kill him – I will.

EPILOGUE

His new home was the woods - the Bluebell Woods - and that's where he resided for the past thirteen years.

He knew Kane was still out there, watching and waiting, waiting to finish what they had started.

He ran away from the old John Brown's shipyard the day that he severed his father's spine. He knew good old daddy dearest was still alive, it was just a matter of time before he finally came looking for him too.

He wasn't scared, wasn't scared of dying and certainly wasn't scared of those two. He lived off the land: eating vegetation and any animals he could catch, deer, cows, badgers, foxes all became meals for him.

This was his home and no one would find him…

…yet.

END.

ACKNOWLEDGEMENTS

It took sixteen years to finally get this story out of my mind and onto paper. I am grateful for the skills, patience and kindness of the team at Spinetinglers, particularly Lauren Neill.

I must also thank my whole family - as mentioned before - for their constant backing of my quest to finally get this story out there.

And lastly to my fans on Facebook who have followed me and read my short stories since 2011, you are all mad.

Thank you to all my family and friends for advice and most importantly for their recommendations of ways to kill people. Keep them coming.

Lightning Source UK Ltd.
Milton Keynes UK
UKOW03f0149141014

240066UK00002B/15/P